THE

Fodder Milo Stories

By Francis Eugene Wood

Frances Eugene Wood 2010

Illustrations by Robert W. McDermott

© 2000 by Francis Eugene Wood, Jr.
Cover art © 2000 by Robert W. McDermott
Illustrations © 2000 by Robert W. McDermott

Published by Tip-Of-The-Moon Publishing Company
Farmville, Virginia

Printed by Farmville Printing
Photograph by Chris Wood
Book design by FEW and Jon Marken

email: fewwords@moonstar.com
website: http://tipofthemoon.com

ISBN: 0-9657047-5-0

Dedicated to little rivers
and old storytellers.

Author's Note

My sincere gratitude is extended to Elizabeth Pickett for her help and guidance in editing this project and to Jeanne Clabough and Scott Ainslie for their advice and support.

Bob McDermott's ability to embrace the character of Fodder Milo with his wonderful artistry has both impressed and inspired this author.

Thanks to Jon Marken and Dan Dwyer at Farmville Printing for their part in bringing this author's vision to fruition.

Last, but not least, I am forever grateful to Chris for her patience and unwavering commitment.

Table of Contents

Introduction

When I was nine years old, I met a man along the banks of the Meherrin River in Brunswick County, Virginia, who loved to do two things: fish and tell stories. His name was Fodder Milo. His mother and father had been slaves, but Fodder was born into a free life. And what a life he had! He'd chased Indians and outlaws out West and helped defeat the Spanish in 1898. I had never heard of a Buffalo Soldier until I met this kind old gentleman. Our shared passions for fishing and storytelling brought us together beneath oaks and river birches on steamy summer days from 1963 until 1966. These were turbulent years for a country racked with the pressures of an unwanted war and civil unrest. The river was our escape from it all. It was there that a boy could put away his fears of the future and listen as an old man told of his past.

When I came to know Fodder, he lived alone. But there had been Bell, his wife of sixty-one years, and their three children. The boys were Shad and Boler, and there was a daughter named Anna. He told me about them in his stories, so I came to know them, also.

Buster, a black and white mixed-breed dog, was Fodder Milo's constant companion. The dog would bark and fetch on command, and he'd perform a little dance when Fodder played the harmonica. I can still recall the sound of the music and the clouds of dust which enveloped the dancing dog.

My grandmother once told me that we are destined to know a few pure souls during our time here. I came to know one in Fodder Milo. Time is a strange bandit, for even as it robs us of our youth, it graces us with wisdom. I realize now that times are never easy for any generation, as each one must bear its share of joy and strife. From Fodder Milo I learned how one can come through it all with dignity and a measure of understanding that hints of other-worldly knowledge.

Fodder once said to me, "One day I'll see my Bell ag'in, an' dat'll be a fine reunion."

He passed away in the fall of 1966 at the age of 94. I grew up and went on with my life, but I have never forgotten him. Grandmother was right. He was a pure soul and a fine gentleman, and he was my good friend.

These stories are from a self-taught man. He told them well, and I listened as a child listens, absorbing every word and inflection. My initial desire was to bring Fodder's stories to the public, using his own Southern Appalachian dialect. The original manuscript for the book retains that uniqueness. However, it is my belief that the stories are much more important than my effort to devise and duplicate his pronunciations. Therefore, I have softened his manner of speech to make a more easily read narrative. The more heavily laden dialect comes in the quotes from passing characters.

I have chosen certain entries from my personal journal (1963-1966) and placed them throughout this book. These serve as a link between the young journalist and the old storyteller.

As for the authenticity of Fodder's tales, I can only say that I never questioned his integrity or his intent. I hope you enjoy the Fodder Milo stories as much as I did.

Author's journal entry for May 25, 1963

My teacher is Mrs. Blick. She's a nice lady and likes me because I'm quiet, and I tell her funny stories at lunchtime. I sit behind Michael Clark. He's my best friend, and his sister, Pat, is my girlfriend. I kissed Pat behind the coal pile yesterday. I hope she wasn't expecting much because I don't think I was too good at it. I might marry her one day if she don't get tired of me. Michael had to stay in at recess today because he drew a man with three legs. Mrs. Blick said men don't have three legs. Everybody wanted to laugh, but didn't. I told Michael he should've drawn a shoe on it. Fodder Milo told me he thinks I might grow eight inches before next summer. That will be good, because Pat is taller than me. That old man knows a lot of stories, and he tells them to me. We've been friends for two weeks now. I found him down on the river fishing for catfish. I never caught a catfish before, but now I'm getting good at it. There's secrets to catching big catfish, and Fodder knows them. He plays an old harmonica a man gave him a long time ago. I might get me one someday.

Music Man

Mamma were in Bradley Murdock's Dry Goods Store one day, when I think I must've been eight or nine year old. It weren't no way I were goin' to be inside long, so I come out on the street and commenced to walkin' around some.

I had about six cent in my pocket until I went to Mr. Ogle's store and bought me some horehound candy for two cent. I did love that horehound candy too much!

I were lookin' at the doodads on the shelves when I heard Mr. Ogle say, "Dee, that damn beggar's back on the street again," and he walked over to the front door and looked right put out. His wife were a fat thing, as I recollect, and she come up front, and poked her puffy face out the door and yelled, "Git on away from here, you!" like she were talkin' to a dog.

It got quiet out front, an' I heard a fella say back to her, "Yes, m'am, I be movin' 'long, now."

Miz Ogle were always boilin' up eggs in the back of the store for a big vinegar jar what set on the counter next to the cash drawer. Them eggs were good, too, and you could have one for a penny. But when she were doin' the boilin', I'd almost lose my taste for one, 'cause the whole place smelt awful.

Well, that mornin', I come out of the Ogles' store and I seen this old fella walkin' up the sidewalk with a guitar swung across his back, and a beat-up suitcase in his hand. Had his hat pushed back on his head, what showed he were gray. But he were sure dressed like a gentleman, even if he were a bit rag-tag. Had a cane, too, and I reckoned he were just about blind.

Now I were a curious boy and commenced to followin' that old man, but he must've heard me, 'cause he stopped after a while and says, "You gots a good little town here, an' duh Lawd done spoke to me 'bout it."

His face were to the sky, but I knew he were talkin' to me. So I says to him, "What'd He say to you?"

That old fella smiled and cocked his head a little and says to me, "Duh Lawd tells me, 'Sing, Bill Henry, sing!'" And with that, he laid into a lively rendition of "Amazing Grace" like I ain't never heard before or since.

When he finished, I says to him, "Yo' name's Bill Henry?"

And he says back, "Sho' is, boy, sho' is!"

I says to him that my name were Fodder Milo, and

he reached out his hand. I can almost feel that hand now, all big and warm. I weren't afraid of Bill Henry none, and I led him across the road to a bench under a oak tree. He were sweatin' right good, so I run down the street and brung him a jar of water from Ben Yoder's livery stable.

When I got back to him, Bill Henry were tunin' his guitar. He drunk a sip of water and licked his lips and says to me, "Thanks, Fodda Milo. You is a good boy to he'p a ol' man."

But I didn't know I were bein' nothin' but curious about what he were doin' in town. And I liked music a lot and couldn't git enough of it.

I sure did enjoy his singin' that day, especially when he played the harmonica, too. I'd tap my feet and clap for him, and he'd just say to me, "You is a good boy, Fodda Milo, to make a stranger feel welcome in yo' little town."

But he weren't like no stranger I ever seen before. It were like I knowed him for a long time.

While he were singin', some people come by and dropped him a nickel or a dime, and he'd thank them.

I sure did like Bill Henry, so when he were singin' to heaven, I give him the only thing I had, and that weren't but four cent.

After a while, I seen Mamma comin' out of the store and I knowed I had to git on. So I says to my friend, "I got to git on, now, but I enjoyed yo' music, Bill Henry."

He smiled and reached out and touched my shoulder and says, "Duh Lawd'll light yo' way, Fodda Milo, an' songs is hear'd in heaven."

I recollect thinkin' that were a strange thing to say, but I kind've understood. Then I said goodbye. I left him singin' on the bench, and he were loud enough to make that old fat Miz Ogle shake her head in the doorway of her store.

A week or so later, I got a package sent from one Bill Henry over in Knoxville. I opened it up, and it were a new harmonica like what he played. I were real thankful and a right proud boy, too! The note what come with it weren't much, and I reckon he got somebody to write it for him. It just said, "Songs is hear'd in heaven, Fodda Milo. The Lawd'll show you how to play. Yo frien', Bill Henry."

Well, I never seen Bill Henry no more in my life, but I ain't never let go of that harmonica. And I can play right many songs on it, too. I reckon Bill Henry knowed a thing or two. I like to think of him playin' for the Lord now. That makes me smile some.

Author's journal entry for July 22, 1963

It rained this morning, but the sun came out after lunch. I went to the river and found that old man catching grasshoppers in the weeds. Buster was with him. Fodder played a tune on his harmonica, and that dog started barking and jumping around. Fodder says he was dancing. I laughed so hard at that dog, and we started stomping around in the weeds. Fodder says I'm half wild, and I told him I got Indian blood in me. So, he says I got a right to be wild. I liked stomping around in the field with Buster, and the grasshoppers were flying everywhere. I like to hear Fodder play the harmonica.

Plowboy

I got to plowin' and tendin' gardens for folks when I got up in size a bit. Now, if you don't think that's hard work, then you ain't been told right, 'cause I done it, and I know.

You got to have a good mule. A good horse'll do, but up in the mountains where I come from, a mule's best, 'cause he's more sure in the hoof. But he can be trouble like you ain't never seen.

I had a mule I called Lem, and he were one fine beast, except for when he set his mind against a thing. Sometimes we'd be goin' along real good and, all of a sudden, he'd stop dead in his tracks and wouldn't go nary a step. Most times I'd be wantin' to finish up, but Lem weren't no fool and must've knowed I weren't able to pull the plow without him. I'd yell and coax him the best I could before I'd walk around in front of him and ask him what were wrong. Sometimes it'd be a dog howlin' off in the hills somewhere, or I might have to kick a rock out of his path. Whatever it were, he'd git over it in a while and git on with it.

I recollect one day it were hot as blazes, and old Miz Johnson up in Widow's Hollow had me and Lem plowin' corn rows on a hill so steep and rocky, you'd about start a landslide every time the plow would turn the soil. I don't think that woman owned a piece of flat land nowhere, but she paid good, about two dollar for half a day's work, and that weren't bad for a poor boy.

When we finished work that day, old Miz Johnson give me money and a fine lookin' hat her dead husband didn't need no more. I were one proud thing hitchin' Lem up to the wagon and sayin' my farewell. Except Lem didn't take to that hat and got to actin' up some, so I took it off and laid it on the seat beside me. Lem were funny like that. Didn't like nothin' unusual, and I didn't usually sport no hat back then.

So we come down off the hill and struck the road to Miz Bracy's farm across Wolf Creek. Lem just poked along, lest I said, "Make tracks, Lem!" and slapped the reins on him. Then he'd poke a little faster.

Wolf Creek is a rocky thing, and when we got to the bridge across it, there were three boys busy at somethin' what looked like no good to me; and I says to Lem, "I see trouble comin'." I recognized the Bowdie twins, Zeke and Edmond, and the other one were a boy I weren't fond of at all named Jake Pott.

About the time we got to the bridge, they were placin' a log across it, and I says to Lem, "Whoa!" But he would've anyway 'cause sometimes a little rock will make him stop dead in his tracks. I nodded and didn't say nothin'.

Then that rascal, Jake, spoke up and says, "Most folks we let pass here without payin', but a plowboy with a mule and a wagon puts a right good strain on this here bridge."

The twins just stood there with their chests puffed out like tusslin' bantams.

I eyeballed them and says, "I ain't never paid to cross this bridge."

And Jake says back, "We weren't here before to charge you." Then he looked back at the Bowdies and smirked, "Now look here, plowboy, we seen ya up at old lady Johnson's, and we know she paid ya, and ya ain't gittin' yerself or that ugly mule across this here bridge lest ya give us somethin'."

Now I were just a boy, but I weren't no fool, and I figured it this way: Them boys were the meanest young' uns in the hills. Their papas were moonshiners, and their mammas weren't the type you'd see at a church social, or tackin' quilts with the fine ladies about town. The only thing them boys got honest were meanness, and they weren't too choosy who they give it to.

So, I, not wantin' to git into it with them, concocted a plan what to git me out of a scrap, while at the same time showin' them a thing. It didn't take me more than a blink to come up with somethin', 'cause I were always quick to figure. "I'll tell you what," I says. "You boys is right to reckon I'd git paid for plowin' Miz Johnson's garden, but she must've forgot to give me the money."

Jake Pott figured I were lyin', and rightly so, but

it weren't none of his business, anyway.

So I sweetened it a little and says, "Tell you what I'm goin' to do. I'm goin' to walk back to Miz Johnson's and git my money, and to show you I'm intendin' to do right, I'll let you take old Lem here on to the Bracy farm, and I'll meet you there and give you somethin'."

Jake looked at Zeke and Edmond, who didn't have much in the way of good sense between them, and asked them what they thought.

Zeke spoke up and says, "Ya don't give us somethin', plowboy, we'll keep yer wagon, yer plow, and yer ugly mule, too!"

Edmond smiled right ornery-like, and Jake says to them, "Come on," and they proceeded to step onto the wagon, as I gave up my seat and stepped down. Of course, I didn't want no one sittin' on my new, fine hat, so I took it down with me.

Jake Pott took the reins and says to me, "Ya best move that log, plowboy, so we can git on to the Bracys'. And don't ya be long, neither."

I nodded to them and says, "Sure will, boys!" Then I waved that hat.

Well, you ain't never seen such a calamity in your life like what happened then. Old Lem reared up and give a holler like the devil were after him and cut down the bank towards the creek. The thing happened so fast, I hardly got to the bridge rail before what were done got did. Them boys were a-screamin' and a-bouncin' all over that wagon when that mule charged down that rocky bank, and that just spooked him, more. Zeke went in the air first, when old Lem jerked that wagon into the creek, and he hit the bank before he rolled on into the water. As I said, Wolf Creek were rocky, and them wagon wheels commenced to doin' a ragged jig across it. It's a good thing old Lem were as sure-footed as he were, or I think he might've went down and got hurt. But he were watchin' out for hisself, even with the daylights scared out of him. He looked kinda perty, splashin' the water and bawlin' and all.

Edmond come out the wagon and about cut his head on the blade of the plow, but it were tied down tight in the back and weren't damaged none. He went headfirst into the creek, and the current rolled him downstream.

Jake Pott were the only one to begin the wild ride up and out of the creek with old Lem, and he were holdin' on for his life. But it weren't no good, 'cause when Lem took to the bank on the far side, he hauled that wagon up with such a speed that Jake lost his grip and tumbled head over heels off the back. And he didn't stop tumblin' until he were face down in Wolf Creek.

Lem come up that bank, wild as the devil, and I says, "Whoa, Lem!" And he did, right soon after he got back up on the road, and just stood there like nothin' happened. I looked down at them boys in that creek, and they were bleedin' and cussin'. I picked up that log on the bridge and made sure they seen me toss it over to the side of the road, 'cause I were right strong, and that were good for them to know.

They didn't say nothin' to me. I set that dead man's hat up on the bridge rail and says to them, "I work hard for what I git, but this here hat were give to me for nothin'. I reckon you can fight over it when you've finished bathin'."

I got up in that wagon and says, "Git on, Lem!" And he did.

Author's journal entry for August 21, 1963

I don't want to go back to school because it's so boring. I like to fish and swim and listen to Fodder's stories. I write what he says in my book, but he don't know it. I would like to have Fodder for my teacher. He'd be a good one. "A" is for apple, "B" is for bobwhite, "C" is for can—if you want to, and "F" is for fishing. He told me never to drink no whiskey or smoke, because if I did, I'd be sorry for it someday. And always be good to people, because you get what you give.

Uncle Jad's Remedy

I were a young man livin' at home with the folks and workin' for wages, when, one day, I come down with the meanest cough I ever had in my life. I were a-hackin' every minute, and Mamma says to me, "If'n ya ain't better 'fo' Sat'dy, ya best git on to yo' Uncle Jad's place an' git ya some rem'dy."

Well, come Saturday, I weren't no better, and it were takin' its toll on my work. So I commenced to hikin' up to Uncle Jad's cabin.

Jad lived way up the mountain in a hollow what belonged to him, and nobody best come up there, lest they were kin to him, or he'd likely make them disappear.

It were widely knowed that Jad were a moonshiner, and he were a bit peculiar. He'd lost his wife in childbirth, but she give him a perty little angel for a daughter that he didn't have no idea what to do with, so my folks took her in. We'd take her up the hollow to see her papa about every two weeks, so he knowed us real good.

Sometimes when I'd be goin' up the trail to his place (it were no wider than a deer run) I'd git right jittery thinkin' somebody were watchin' me. When I'd git to Jad's place, he'd be sittin' on the porch, a-rockin' in his chair and smokin' his pipe. And the first thing he'd say were, "I knowed ya was comin'."

I says, "How'd you know that, Uncle?"

And he says, "Duh woods said it to me."

And I'd believe him, 'cause he'd know the tune I were whistlin' and how many times I'd stumbled along the way.

Uncle Jad were a bit of a healer, too. But when he couldn't do nothin' to save his wife, he lost some faith; and a healer's got to have faith or else healin's a chore.

I knowed him to blow the colic from a baby, and to rub warts off your hands, but he'd stopped all that after his wife passed on. Since then, his healin' were in concoctions, what all seemed to center around moonshine. It were against the law to sell moonshine, so Jad called it "rem'dy" and sold it off right good. Most everybody had some of Jad's remedy for sickness and such.

Well, Uncle Jad thumped my chest and says, "1 hears a rattlin' in dar." He give me a jar of remedy and says, "Jest sip twice't a day, or it'll knock mo' out o' ya den dat rattle."

I agreed, and after I'd caught him up on the gossip down the mountain, I left him on the porch, as usual, with his pipe and chair and shotgun.

About half-way down that mountain, I got to hackin' right good, 'til I had to sit down and catch my breath. While I were restin', I lifted the lid of that jar and took me a little sip. It weren't bad goin' down, but before it hit bottom, a fire rose up in me what made my eyes water and my nose burn somethin' fierce. I hacked a little and got better right quick, so I commenced to take my second sip of the day right there, thinkin' this weren't bad at all if it could work so fast. The second sip went down the same as the first and sent a fire up after it, but I didn't mind much, 'cause the hackin' done gone, and I about danced off that mountain.

I felt so fine, I decided to go to the village for some socializin'. By the time I come to town, it were gittin' dark, but I didn't care none. I were one happy customer and would've walked off a cliff with a smile on my face!

Now there's one thing for sure about one that's happy with drink, and that's the fact that he's happier with people nearby. So I figured to find me a friend. Just before I come onto Main Street, I heard a man singin' a tune, and when I followed his voice, I found me a friend sittin' on the broken-down porch of the old Tutor cabin. Them Tutors had been gone a long time, and people said their place were hainted.

But my new friend weren't afraid, and when he seen me comin', he says, "Howdy, friend!" And he shook my hand 'til I thought he weren't goin' to stop. He were the smilin'est white man I'd ever seen, and he says to me, "I'm Bob, an' who are you?"

I told him who I were. I were sure he were

one drunk customer, but he were friendly as a soul could be, and we got along real good.

Now Bob were a fine singer, and when he heard me play my harmonica, he about swallowed the bottle he were suckin' on. I could play all the good tunes, and Bob sang every word to them. He wanted to know what I were drinkin', and I says, "I ain't drinkin' nothin', Bob. Just remedy."

And he laughed like it were a big lie.

Bob had a idea that we find us some ladies down on Black Gum Road, on the other side of town. I weren't against it 'cause I were single at the time and didn't know no better.

Bob and me made a right happy pair walkin' down Main Street, and we might've made it over to Black Gum Road, too, if it weren't for the fact that we'd done got loud, what with the playin' and singin' and all.

Before I knowed it, we were stopped by a big old fat policeman. He said somethin' what must've riled old Bob, 'cause Bob says to him, "I'll see you in Court, Manus Lee!"

But after that, we got took down to the police station, and Bob says to me, "Don't you worry none, Fodder Milo. I'll take care of everything." And he laughed.

But I weren't laughin' much no more, 'cause

Manus Lee done pushed me right hard.

That remedy of Uncle Jad's would do funny things to your mind, and I think I passed out. When I woke up, I were in jail, feelin' real poorly. I ain't never been in no jail before then, and I were right ashamed. The jailer man were nice, and he said he knowed my folks and would call on them for me.

It were right lonely in that jail cell. The jailer man said he didn't know no drunk named Bob, so I just waited to see the judge that afternoon.

Well, when I stood in front of that bench and heard that voice say to me, "How do you plead, Fodder Milo? Guilty or innocent?" I just hung my head and knowed I were a pure fool. That judge sounded a mighty lot like Bob to me, and his eyes were about as bloodshot as mine!

He says, "This Court finds you guilty of public intoxication and sentences you to two days in the County Jail and a ten-dollar fine."

Well, I done my time and I paid the fine. To this day, I ain't never seen the inside of no jail again, 'cause it were a shameful thing to me. I also learned a lesson or two about people and drinkin' that I ain't never forgot.

Author's journal entry for June 16, 1964

Today, while I was sitting on the steps in front of church, Rita C. told me she loved me. I told her she's been watching too much TV. Rodney Elmore says she's pretty, but I won't tell him what she said, because I'd never hear the end of it. I don't understand girls too much. One day they love you, and the next, they're making faces at you. I just don't talk to them much, because I don't know what to say to them. I like Margaret, though, because she's not like a real girl. We've been friends all our lives, and she likes to run in the wild woods with me. Fodder Milo told me about a girl he knew named Renny Martin. She was something.

Slippery Rocks

In the summer of my sixteenth year, I learned somethin' about women and preachers.

One day when I were fishin' for trout at my favorite hole in Wolf Creek, I heard a gigglin' behind me, and when I turned around, I seen it were Renny Martin.

Now Renny were a perty thing, and she were in full bloom in all the right places. But she were touched by somethin' what made her giggle at you and recite the silliest verses you ever heard. She were also real friendly with the boys around to where a lot of them knowed her in a right familiar way.

"What ya doin, Fodda Milo?" she says to me that day.

And I says, "Fishin', Renny."

"Well," she says, "I seen ya pass by duh house, an' I figga'd ya'd be comin' here." With that, she come over and sat down beside me, and she smelled like a flower garden.

I weren't never no lady's man, even when I were a boy, so I says to her, "Renny, these here fish ain't bitin' too good today."

She just giggled some. "Fishin' an' wishin' don't make no man, Fodda."

But I acted like I didn't hear her. Even when she sat down beside me, I tried to pay her no mind, 'cause I knowed she weren't right. It were a hard thing not to look at that girl, and she smelled so good and all. I says to her, "What you come here for, Renny?"

But she didn't say one word. She just got up against me and blowed on my neck a little.

Well, my pole got to shakin' somethin' fierce, and weren't a fish in sight!

Renny took that pole out of my hands and says again, "Fishin' an' wishin' don't make no man, Fodda Milo."

I didn't catch supper that evenin' like I usually done, and when my mamma says to me, "Where's supper, Fodda?"

I says back, "Weren't bitin' today, Mamma." But I couldn't look her in the eye, and I weren't hungry, neither.

I went for a walk and ended up at my favorite tree overlookin' Banger's Hollow where I killed my first bear. A breeze were stirrin', and I leaned against the bole of that big fat pine and had me a talk with the Lord. I don't know if He heard me, 'cause the wind were gittin' up some, and there were a coon dog barkin' in the bottom. But I do recollect feelin' a little better when I started home.

Life is a funny thing, 'cause sometimes when you think you is gittin' on to one thing, another one comes up and gives you a snag.

When I come back home that evening, I heard

some talkin' in the kitchen, and Mamma called to me, "Fodda, come in here and say 'How-do' to Reveren' Scruggs."

Well, she could've said, "Fodda, duh Reveren' Scruggs been watchin' ya t'day an' gots sump'm to say 'bout it!" and it wouldn't affected me no different! My heart come up and commenced to hammerin' in my throat, and I couldn't swallow it back down for nothin'!

If old St. Peter could give you a judgmental stare at the Pearly Gates, it couldn't be nothin' more than that cockeyed look from the Reverend Scruggs. He were one sour individual, if ever I knowed one. I'd describe him as a squat stump of a man, with a great big belly. He were graying some when I knowed him, but he weren't too old. Had big bushy eyebrows what made him look kind of silly, and he really were cockeyed. They say he got hisself poked in the eye when he were a young 'un out huntin' coons, and that the muscles what controlled his right eyeball didn't heal up right. So if he were lookin' at you straight on, that right eyeball would be wanderin' off somewhere else. It were strange to talk to him, 'cause sometimes you'd think he were watchin' more than a few things at once.

I knowed one thing about him, and I weren't alone, neither. It were a fact that he'd eyeball the ladies more than a preacher ought to. Some of the menfolk in the Wolf Creek Baptist Church wouldn't allow their wives to invite the Reverend to drop by, unless they were home. It were a joke to some, but others couldn't see past his white collar, and that were the cleanest thing about him, I reckon.

When I walked into the kitchen, he didn't stand up or nothin', just says to me, "Well, Fodda, yo' mamma says you is quite the fisherman," and I nodded my head a little. Then he says to me, "Duh Lawd loves a fisherman, boy," and he started quoting the Scriptures. He were just preachin' like it were Sunday morning.

I stood there watchin' that cockeyed look of his and wonderin' where he were goin' with it all.

Then he took a sip of tea and says to me, "I come here to git yo' soul fo' duh Lawd, Fodda. Will ya come into His fold?"

Somewhere in all his talkin' I had a hunch he were after somethin', so I says back to him, "I ain't ready yet for no dippin', Reverend."

Well, he got a little huffy after that, 'cause the annual baptizin' were comin' up Sunday, and he liked to brag to the congregation on all the sheep he done gathered up for the Lord. I'd been to some dippin's, but I weren't too impressed, 'cause I knowed most of them what got dipped in Wolf Creek, and they weren't no better, far as I could see.

The Reverend preached a little more that day, and then says to me, "If ya change yo' heart, I'll be obliged to bring ya into duh Lawd's fold on Sunday. Think about it real hard, Fodda, fo' duh Lawd will come like a thief in duh night."

I were thinkin' "Yep, Reverend, just like you

come around to Blanch Rutter's house one night when her man, Ben, were sellin' cows over in Sevierville." But I didn't say nothin', except, "I'll think on it."

Mamma didn't say much after he'd gone 'cause she knowed I didn't think much of him, and Papa didn't like him at all. Sister Kate didn't never like to be in the room with him, neither. She said Reverend Scruggs were always lookin' at her bosoms, but she didn't tell Mamma that. Mamma just looked for the good in everybody.

When Sunday come, we all gathered at the swimmin' hole at Wolf Creek and heard a sermon under the shade of the oaks and birches. It were right nice, as I recollect, 'cause I didn't like being walled in on Sundays when the sun were shinin'.

A lot of folks I knowed were there for a dippin', and the Reverend Scruggs were about to git at it when along steps Renny Martin. I heard a fella next to me whisper, "Good Lawd!" and his wife shoved her elbow in his side and give him one hard look. I thought to myself, "That girl do look good!" She were smilin' real big when she made her way through the congregation what were standin' and sittin' along the banks of the creek. Everybody were real surprised to see Renny there for a dippin', 'cause they all thought they knowed somethin' about her what were sinful. But I just reckoned the Lord wanted us all.

Renny were dressed out simple, but it didn't

matter. She were wearin' a white linen dress what fit her real nice. Shoot, she were about to bust out of it up top, and she didn't wear no shoes, neither. She done put a wildflower in her hair what were pulled up in a bun. And that were it!

While folks were gaspin' and whisperin', Renny held her head high and took her place among them what were waitin' to be saved.

When Reverend Scruggs seen that girl, he smiled kind of funny-like and shouted, "Praise duh Lawd! I got Ya another un!" He waved for the crowd to come in closer and then waded into the water. I wondered about him, though, 'cause I'd done swum Wolf Creek enough to know that where he were headin' cradled some right slippery rocks. He stumbled a time or two but seemed to find a foothold, and before long, he'd done saved three souls. Each time one went down for a dip, they'd

come up to "Hallelujahs" and "Amens," and they'd come out of that cold water steppin' high!

Then it were time for Renny to git saved, and she had a time wadin' out to the Reverend. She were slippin' real bad on them slick rocks. The poor thing went down once, and when she come up, it were clear to everybody that there weren't nothin' under that perty little dress but skin! Some eyes got to poppin' real good, 'cause the Lord done built that girl real fine. I had to hide a grin when I seen the look on old Reverend Scruggs' face when he seen what must've been a real sight, 'cause that water were cold as ice, and she were about to poke out of that dress, for sure!

The Reverend slipped a little and reached for Renny's hand. For a wink it looked like they were steady, but I think the Reverend were a little too far out, and the current must've sucked on him some, 'cause no sooner than Renny caught on to him, the two of them went down, and all we seen were hands and feet a-flailin' as they spun off in the current.

Well, they were strugglin' right hard, but the current were such that it rolled them over for quite a ways. The congregation stood there gazin' for a while, then somebody says, "Dey's gonna drown!" And Lester Pugh started in after them, but his wife were hollerin' at him, sayin', "Lester, ya cain't swim!" And reminded of that fact, Lester stopped in knee-deep water. Everybody else knowed not to git into the current on that stretch of water.

So we commenced to followin' them two poor souls down the creek and hollerin' at them to grab hold of somethin'.

Finally the Reverend were able to grab a sharp rock. The water were shallow where he were, and he struggled to git a foothold so he could fetch Renny when she come by. Poor Renny were gittin' tossed over right hard, and one time before she got to the Reverend, she come under a fallen tree. I hoped she'd grab onto a limb, but she didn't. She just went under, and when she come up again, the Reverend grabbed her by the hair on her head. She were gaspin' for air and hollerin' somethin', but there were so much water in her mouth, nobody could tell what she were sayin'.

Me and some others waded out and were able to reach the Reverend's hand, and we yanked him hard and got him up and out of the current. Then he pulled Renny up to where we finally seen more than her head. I reckon that fallen tree must've snagged her right good, 'cause I ain't lyin' a bit when I say that she weren't wearin' nothin' but that wildflower in her hair, and it were right crooked. I mean that poor girl were plumb naked as a newborn baby, but Renny weren't no baby! And when she stood up in knee-deep water and raised her hands to heaven and shouted, "I is saved!" well, Miz Melba Goins flat out fainted, and her husband, Ned, didn't see her go down, 'cause he were busy gittin' a eye-full of Renny Martin. I heard Earl Willis say out loud, "Hallelujah, sweet Jesus!"

There were other things bein' said I cain't repeat. But I'm here to tell you that the folks in that congregation were a helpful bunch, 'cause I ain't never in my life seen more fellas willin' to help a poor soul as what I seen come to the aid of Renny Martin that day.

And Reverend Scruggs were doin' all he could, too, what with holdin' her from fallin' back into the current.

I reckon the Reverend and Renny got washed of their sins that day. I think about it sometimes and I laugh a little. I ain't never seen nobody a-slippin' and a-slidin' on rocks more than them two.

I didn't git saved 'til later on, 'cause it took me a while to work things out. Didn't take the dippin' in Wolf Creek, neither, but I reckon I come across some slippery rocks along the way. Most folks do.

Author's journal entry for June 28, 1964

Fodder says he stole a watermelon when he was young, and he's still sorry about it. I told him that I took a little squirt gun from the dime store when I was little, but Jesus was so hard on me, I had to return it. I never would tell my mamma that, because she says I need religion, anyway. But if I get any more religion, I think I'll become a monk, because I can't do nothing bad without feeling guilty. I killed a moccasin snake yesterday, bigger around than my leg. I smelled him before I saw him, and he was so close he could have bit me. So I guess God likes me a little, or I'd be dead now.

Melons and Moccasins

One summer before I were eighteen, I went down to Georgia to visit with my cousin, Fiddle Moody. He were the oldest son of my mamma's sister, Aunt Janey, and her husband, Pud. If you're wonderin' where his folks come up with a name like Fiddle, I'll tell you.

Uncle Pud were part Injun, or at least he said so, and it were a custom to name your children after a sign what come to you at the birth of the baby. I ain't too sure about all that, but I recollect Pud were a boozer, and I heard him say, once when he were two shades to the wind, that a fiddle were the second thing he seen when that boy were born, and he laughed right sly-like so I reckoned it were best that Fiddle be happy about his name. If his papa held to custom, it might've been worse. Fiddle were a wild one if I ever knowed one, and we had us some times back then.

One day we were workin' a field for Mista Maynard Dooley. It were hot as blazes. Mista Dooley were a strange fella, and he didn't like you to rest or nothin' when you were earnin' wages from him. So me and Fiddle were about to thirst to death. I bet between the two of us we sweat enough salt to cure a pig.

When we'd finished that day, old Dooley give us less than a dollar apiece for what we done, and it weren't right. I were happy just to let it go, but Fiddle had a temper, and he says to me as we were walkin' out the field, "We'll show dat ol' fool sump'm, Fodda."

And I says to him, "Just let it go, Fiddle."

But weren't no use to argue with that boy, 'cause he were bent to trouble sometimes.

Now if there were one thing old Dooley were knowed for, it were the melons he growed. They were big and tasty, and he were fond of sellin' them to the market in the village where he turned a good profit.

"We is gonna git us a melon, Fodda," says Fiddle.

And I'm thinkin' to myself, "Old Dooley keeps an eye on that garden of his with a loaded shotgun at the door."

But Fiddle weren't thinkin' nothin' of that, and he laid down a plan for us to git paid in full for our labor.

So that night, we come back and got into old Dooley's melon patch and plucked us two of the biggest ones I ever saw. I could barely tote mine, and got to laughin', 'cause Fiddle were littler than me, and he were a-strugglin' with a melon what made him look like David holdin' up Goliath!

We were doin' good, too, 'til Fiddle, who were

barefoot, stepped on a sharp rock and cussed too loud, and got the dog to barkin' at us.

Well, no sooner than he started up, old Dooley comes out the house a-rantin', and I seen a gun barrel shinin' off the light of his lantern. I says, "Run!" and me and Fiddle commenced to high-tailin' it out of that melon patch. We jumped a rail fence, but I don't know how, 'cause them melons were heavy and awkward, to boot. I looked back and seen that lantern light a-swingin', and old Dooley a-rantin', and I knowed we were in a heap of trouble. "We got to drop these here melons, Fiddle!" I says, as we were a-runnin' side by side.

And he says, "Ain't goin' to do it, Fodda. Head to duh hole!"

And I recollect thinkin' I wished I were back home in the hills. But it weren't no use 'cause I were in it thick, and old Dooley were goin' to kill me for sure for stealin' a darn melon I could've done without.

I looked back and thought, for an old man, he were comin' on right good. "He's goin' to shoot us, Fiddle, if we don't git on," I says as best I could, all out of breath.

Fiddle says back, "Let's jump in duh fishin' hole an' hide unda duh bank. Come on!"

And he led the way, but I knowed it were my last run, 'cause if I followed that fool cousin of mine into that swamp hole, I might as well kiss myself goodbye. It weren't no doubt that the snakes in there would eat us up! I'd seen them—big, fat things. As big around as your leg, and a mouth white like cotton. Fiddle fished that swamp hole all his life and knowed it real good. Said he weren't scared of no moccasin snake, neither, but I knowed he were a fool, sometimes, runnin' around barefoot like he did and all.

About the time I were thinkin' about not gittin' in that black water, old Dooley fired a shot, and I heard the lead hit the leaves on the trees in front of us. Then, we come into the forest, and I fell in behind Fiddle. Before I knowed it, we done plunged into the fishin' hole where snakes big as your leg were waitin'. We were spittin' and spinnin' around looking for the right place to hide, and Fiddle says, "Dar 'tis! Come on!"

I followed him, and we pushed up under the bank as far as we could and got real quiet. I said a prayer to Jesus, but I knowed that He weren't goin' to help no melon thief. I were on my own.

It didn't take old Dooley long to git to the swamp bank, and he commenced to searchin' around with that lantern. You could see it shinin' on the water and lightin' up the eyes of bullfrogs and such. But I knowed some were what belong to a big, fat, mean old snake just waitin' to git under that black water and bite my legs. I were about scared to death, and then I heard a snickerin' and I says, "You best shut up that snickerin', Fiddle."

But he couldn't stop, even when old Dooley were standin' right above us with his shotgun. Then I knowed Fiddle were one wild thing, temptin' death like he were.

Thank the Lord old Dooley couldn't hear him, and after a spell, he cussed us good and skedaddled back to his house. "Let duh snakes have at ya, den," he said. "Ya'll git back in my melon patch ag'in, I'll blast ya to hell!"

He were sore, for sure. But I reckon he didn't know it were us what took his melons.

We huddled there for a good while after old Dooley left. The bullfrogs were a-croakin', and the cool, black water were a-slappin' at my chin.

Fiddle says, "Fodda, ya ev'a been bit by a snake?"

And that were about all I could take. So I pushed my melon out in front of me and come up out of that smelly snake den. It were all I could do to git that melon up on the bank, but when I did, I says to Fiddle, "You ain't kin to no Injun, boy, 'cause Injuns ain't so dumb as to git caught up in a thing like this!"

Fiddle just laughed it off and says, "Nev'a said I were no Injun, an' ain't no Injun nev'a been cheated by Maynard Dooley, or he would'a been scalped, I reckon!"

We went on home, and them melons did taste real fine. But it weren't right stealin them, even from old Dooley.

Me and Fiddle had us a few more good times that summer before I went back home. I were right fond of him in the long run, even if he didn't always do right.

When Fiddle were twenty-four, he got hisself lynched to a oak tree beside his house by the Klan. All he were guilty of were gittin' black folks together so they could vote. It weren't right at all, and his little children seen it, too.

I try to remember good things about Fiddle, and I smile sometimes when I remember his snickerin' in that fishin' hole with old Dooley a-rantin' and a-ravin'. That were a memory, for sure.

Author's journal entry for July 24, 1964

Fodder always sits under the same old tree when he fishes. He says it's a maple more then twice his age, and he's old. I caught more fish than Fodder today. I got stung by a bee, and Fodder put tobacco juice on it. Then he told me a story about his brother, Denton. He was a soldier and fought Indians out West. I told Fodder I wouldn't be able to fight Indians because I got a little Indian blood in me, and I wouldn't fight my people. But he said when you're a soldier, you got to follow orders. When I watch the TV news almost every night, I see dead soldiers who followed orders. I don't think I want to be a soldier, because killing has to make a man feel bad inside his heart, and dying is hard on your family.

Bees'll Sting Ya

Brother Denton were one fine siblin', for sure, and there's been many a time I wished we'd been closer in age. But he were born about eighteen years before I come along, and by the time I could put on my own britches, he were gone.

Denton Milo come into this world a slave, but when he were eleven, he got freed along with everybody else.

Sister Kate told me that when he were a young'un, he were about wild as you can git and not live in a cave or a hole in a tree. Seems Denton didn't much like bein' no slave to nobody, and I cain't blame him for that, 'cause it were wrong then as it is now, and I figured it would've ended even without no war.

Anyway, Denton sharecropped with my papa 'til he come into his fifteenth year, and then he went up North for a better try at it. But the North didn't want no black folk comin' in and workin' or livin' near them, so he joined up with the Army and got hisself sent out West where he worked at buildin' forts and trackin' Injuns.

Now if you don't think that boy could track, you don't know nothin', 'cause everybody said he could trail a ant in a dust storm. But I don't know about that, except he must've been good at it, or it wouldn't got told.

Denton rode with the Tenth U.S. Cavalry. They were all black boys, and some of them done fought in the Civil War. The Injuns called them Buffalo Soldiers and had a right good respect for them, too!

Denton were in on capturin' Geronimo, but he didn't git no credit for that. He tracked down some real mean outlaws, too. Sister Kate said he didn't like killin' Injuns, 'cause he felt sorry for them, and he quit soldierin' 'cause of it.

Denton got him a wife named Lucy, and a little farm in Montana. He lived all right 'til he died in 1931.

I remember something we done when he come home once. I were about six. Denton and me and Cousin Lee, who didn't have more than a lick of sense, were huntin' squirrels for supper when we seen a big old hornet's nest hangin' in a tree, right over our heads.

Denton says to us, "Now, y'ens be quiet, 'cause a bee don't like no loud talk none!" Then, while we were lookin' up at them bees, he says, "If'n a swarm ev'a gits at ya, ya best run hard, 'cause dem bees'll sting ya sump'm fierce!"

About then, Cousin Lee pipes up and says, "Well, my Aint Jessy says if'n dey gits at ya, all ya gots to do is lay down flat and dey'll pass ya by."

I didn't know about that, and Denton shook his head and says, "You is one crazy boy, Lee!"

We'd a-walked away from there right then, except for the reason that Cousin Lee were right much of a fool, and he throwed a stick up and hit that hornet's nest, and it come down hard on us.

I ain't tellin' nothin' wrong when I says that the devil hisself couldn't a-sent no rain from hell no hotter then them bees were after us. We commenced to runnin' fast as we could, and they were right on us when Lee hollers, "Lay down!" and he dropped to the ground on his face.

But me and Denton were hightailin' it, and Denton hollered back, "Ya betta git yo'se'f up, Lee!"

I were in agreement with my brother, and we run like the devil were about to git us, 'til we heard Lee screamin' for help. We stopped, 'cause there weren't no bees after us no more. They were too busy stingin' Lee!

Denton cussed a little and says to me, "Ya stay still, Fodda," and I did. He cut a limb from a maple tree and went back and beat the hornets off our fool cousin.

Denton had to carry that boy back to his folk's house, 'cause he were one hurtin' fool and swelled up like a bloated varmint.

Lee got better, but he never did git no smarter. A few years later, he got hisself killed while nappin' on a railroad track.

Denton and me laughed about them bees later, but he were serious when he says to me before he went back to fightin' Injuns, "Now, Fodda, if'n ya gits yo'se'f in a fix ag'in wit' bees, ya best run fast as ya can, 'cause bees'll sting ya sump'm fierce."

I ain't never forgot them words.

I met a fella from Buckingham what rode with Denton in the Tenth. His name were Goolsby. He says to me once, "Yo' brotha was a brave man, an' he saved my hide from duh Injuns once't when we were pinned down an' I'd been wounded. Denton Milo took down five o' dem, an' two o' dem in han'-to-han' fightin'."

I knowed that my brother done seen some hard times and been in some right fierce fights, but I knowed his heart, too, and he weren't fond of killin' no Injuns. He said to me once, "Duh red man's like us, Fodda, jest wantin' to be free to go his way."

I understood them words better the older I got.

Author's journal entry for August 2, 1964

Today, Fodder told me about when he met his wife. He said he never saw a girl so pretty in all his life. He was a soldier then and knew Teddy Roosevelt. I wish I knew a great man like that, but they don't live here unless I count my dad and Fodder. But nobody knows they are great but me. I want to meet a girl one day if I don't go and die in Vietnam. Every time I watch the news I see dead soldiers, and I don't even know why they're dying. I wonder if they do.

Courtin' Bell

The first time I seen Bell she were fifteen, and I were about ten year older. I'd gone out to Montana in '90, and against the wishes of my brother, Denton, I'd hitched up with the cavalry and found myself trackin' renegades what couldn't seem to keep to the reservations. I don't blame them red men none, 'cause the government had them livin' poorly, for sure. I brung in enough of them that I got a reputation for trackin'.

Once, I done tracked a renegade about to his bed, when I heard a twig snap behind me. When I turned, he were comin' for me with a knife in his hand. Well, I jumped out the way just in time and somehow kicked that knife out of his grip. He didn't have no other weapon on him, and my pistol were jammed, so we went at it, hand-to-hand. I swear that Injun were strong as a wildcat, and me and him about

beat the tar out of each other before we ended up on our knees, weak as kittens from battlin'. He come at me once more, and fell flat on his face.

Well, I got to thinkin' how silly we were and started a-grinnin'. I reckon he thought I were goin' to finish him. When he seen I weren't, he grinned back at me! We ended up shakin' hands and sharin' vittles! He were Comanche, and I knowed some of his words, so we talked a while, and he said the Army done killed his wife and children. His name meant "Big Cloud." I didn't take him in 'cause he were a good man, and all he wanted were to be free. I knowed, for sure, then that Denton were right about Injuns.

It weren't long after that the Army got itself into a bad thing and killed a passel of Injuns, including women and children, at a place called Wounded Knee. I weren't in on that, but I come up on it the next day, and were ordered to help with the buryin'. It were the worst thing I ever seen, and it were wrong. A lot of soldiers knowed it were wrong, but they got caught by fear. The officers told us to shut up about it all or we'd see trouble. Well, it were wrong all the way!

Later, when I were on leave, I come back East. That's when I were home for a while, and went to a church social and seen Bell Wintree. Oh, she were perty as a picture, and all the young fellas were interested in her. I weren't no lady's man, but I'm told I looked right fine in a uniform, and when I were introduced as Fodder Milo, of the Tenth U.S.

Cavalry, she paid me some attention. We talked a while, and I asked to see her if I could. I were a happy man when she said yes.

Over the next three weeks, we come to know each other real good. I'd pick wild flowers for her, and we'd sit out under the stars at night and tell about each other. She were smart and done read books I ain't never heard of. She told me book stories, and I told her about things I'd done. She'd laugh at me 'cause, mostly, I told her the silly things.

Me and Bell got along real good, and every time I seen her, my heart would git to pumpin' fast! She wrote me poems, and I recall one what went:

Until the wind does cease to blow
Or desert sands turn to snow,
I'll love thine heart and cherish thine kiss,
And when alone, thine love I'll miss...

Bell must've seen somethin' in me, 'cause before I left for duty, she said she'd marry me when I come home. It were hard to leave her, but I had to finish up what I'd started, and the Army were a-callin'.

Bell were at the train station in Sevierville when I pulled out, and she give me that poem I recited. I'll never forget the tears on her perty face when we said goodbye.

It weren't long before I were on a ship bound for Cuba, 'cause the government done got itself in another scrap.

Author's journal entry for August 21, 1964

Fodder Milo fought the Indians and Spanish, but he won't tell me if he killed any. I don't blame him because if he bragged about it, then I'd think he was messed up inside. He laughed at me today when I built a raft and it broke to pieces in the river. I swallowed about a quart of river water. Fodder said, "Don't go drownin', 'cause I don't want to git my shoes wet a-fetchin' ya." We went to his house, and had milk and cornbread. I showed him how my Grandpa Clabo and my Uncle Howard sop their cornbread in a glass of milk before they eat it. Fodder said he'd been doing that all his life. I like his house, because it's old, and he has a lot of neat stuff in it. I'd like to stay at Fodder's house sometimes, but I know Mamma wouldn't let me. I don't ever tell my folks about me and Fodder. Folks are funny about that, but I don't see why because most of the kids I know have been half-raised by black ladies. And I love Mandy Goodrich like she is my own blood. She's got a goiter on her neck. I like it when she sings to me because that old woman knows the best songs. She says Jesus is going to be here in the bat of an eye. But I bat my eyes a hundred times a day, and I haven't seen Him yet.

Soldierin'

By the spring of 1898 I'd been a soldier for a right good spell, and I done seen a lot more than I cared to. I'd ridden guard for settlers what knowed nothin' about life in the West. I'd protected them from Injuns and bears and, mostly, themselves, just to have many of them treat me like a dog. But I were followin' orders and went on with it. I done blazed trails and hunted buffalo and bear and put up more telegraph lines and bridges than you can shake a stick at. And I reckon I'd a-kept it up, except for the fact that Bell Wintree were on my mind. So I figured I'd have me one more military adventure before I packed it in. Boy, I didn't know nothin'!

We sailed on to Siboney, near Santiago, around the 22nd of June, and I recollect it were about time, too, 'cause I were about seasick as a fella could git, and I weren't alone. Most of the black regiments been yanked out of the West, and we were supposed to be leadin' the fight, but we were in a sickly way for a while.

Once we got our feet on dry land, we come around. We put up camps, and for once, had at some decent vittles. I were fixin' biscuits one mornin' when I heard a fella say, "Are you Fodder Milo, sir?"

I looked up and saw it were Lt. Colonel Teddy Roosevelt hisself, and I says to him, "Yes, sir, if he ain't been killed yet, I reckon I am!"

He laughed and slapped me on the back and says, "Bully!"

Then he got to eyeballin' my biscuits, and I says, "You want somethin', Sir?" I knowed he did, cause he'd tasted my biscuits before back in 1895, out in Montana when I'd done guided him right on to a big old bear he killed with one fine shot. He remembered that bear, but it were second to my biscuits!

We sat there a good while and bumped gums about things, and he says to me, "Fodder, you're a good soldier, and I'm proud to have you alongside."

That were a nice thing to hear, 'cause the black regiments didn't git much in the way of praise. But we were some hard men, and they all knowed it. Shoot, the first time I ever seen white and black soldiers conferrin' much were in Cuba. It were a good thing to see, 'cause we didn't have nobody but us.

Fever were killin' us more than Spanish bullets, and a decision were made to git it over quick.

About July 1st, General Shafter led a full charge against Santiago, with about half his men goin' against the Spanish fort at El Caney, and the other half goin' up on Kettle Hill and San Juan Hill.

Now don't git me wrong here, 'cause I thought the world of my friend, Teddy Roosevelt, but I'm goin' to have to tell you the story accordin' to what *I* seen, and here it is:

Colonels Wood and Roosevelt busted up the force to take Kettle Hill where the Spanish were holdin' real stubborn-like. They had them a lot of men and guns up there, and it were a sure thing we would lose some men in the charge.

The main charge got to goin' with Colonel Roosevelt in the lead, just a-shoutin' and a-wavin' his gun. He were a sight, for sure, and were good at gittin' the men aroused. Some of the 10th Cavalry were with him, but me and the rest were sent around to flank the charge in case it got bogged down. Well, it did!

About halfway up Kettle Hill, the firin'

from them Spanish got so hot, the Americans commenced to diggin' in and huggin' the dirt. Lots of them met their Maker that day, but they were as fearless a bunch as I ever seen. They were tryin' to inch up the hill when Sergeant Jones says to me, "Fodda, it's about time." Just then I noticed a soldier named Billy Davis, what were real nervous, throwin' rocks at a hornet's nest in the tree we were huddlin' under. I remembered that day when the bees got after me and Denton and that fool, Cousin Lee. Well, I just got myself up and commenced to movin' on out of there real fast. It were a good thing, too, 'cause Davis hit the nest, and it come down in the middle of us, with the bees just a-swarmin'!

Sergeant Jones hollered, "Wait a minute!"

But the men done trampled him to git away from them bees, and he give up and hollered, "Charge, then, dammit!"

Well, we were chargin', all right, and a-jumpin', and a-hollerin' like a bunch of Injuns, 'cause bees'll sting you somethin' fierce, if you go messin' with them.

Them Spanish got right bewildered when we come at them out of nowhere, and that give Colonels Roosevelt and Wood a chance to strike another charge.

We just outdid them Spanish, and they commenced to runnin' and givin' up. Before I knowed it, we done routed them and took both Kettle Hill and San Juan Hill. The Americans lost a lot of good men that day, but it were a glorious battle, even if it were short.

That were about it, 'cept for a few more skirmishes. In the end, the United States won some islands but passed on keepin' Cuba, and I wondered about that, 'cause there were lots of blood shed over there. It don't make no sense to try and figure about war and all, 'cause, sometimes in the end, you're left wonderin' what you fought for.

The Tenth and the other black regiments were commended for their bravery by most of the officers, and Colonel Roosevelt found me and says, "Fodder, the Tenth was just 'Bully' at Kettle Hill." And he shook my hand.

We were all real happy, and nobody said nothin' about no bee's nest. I reckon that's best.

Anyway, I sailed home in the fall of 1898, set on packin' away my uniform, 'cause I done my fightin', and weren't nothin' on my mind 'cept gittin' back to a perty little girl I left in Tennessee.

Author's journal entry for July 15, 1965

Fodder says he got married in 1899 and went to Montana on his honeymoon. Now he lives alone, but I'm his friend. We took a walk in the woods today, and I think he knows the name of every tree. I want to live in the woods one day, in a log cabin. My wife will have to understand that. Fodder says I'm half wild, and I better tell that to the girl I'm going to marry. I don't know if that's a good idea, because I like the wild woods and the river, and, one day, I'm going to find some bears up in the mountains. And no woman I know likes bears much.

Honeymoonin'

Bell and me got married in the spring of 1899. It were one of the finest days in my life. She were so perty and sweet.

My mamma says to me, "Now, Fodda, ya been taught right, an' ya best be good to dat gal." Mamma hugged on me and were cryin' and all. She were one happy woman.

Before Bell and me left Tennessee for a little trip, my papa says to me, "Fodda, yo' mamma done worried 'bout ya ev'a since ya went off a-soldierin'. Whenev'a duh mail come, she know'd ya'd been kil't."

I didn't figure 'til then how much my folks done fretted about me. But I come back like I said I would, and they were happy when I told them Bell and me were goin' to marry.

There were lots of folks at the weddin', and my friend, Aubrey Butler, who were wounded at Kettle Hill, showed up and give me and Bell a present like I never expected in all my life.

Aubrey were the son of a white timber man over in Virginia near the North Carolina border. When his papa died, Aubrey come into a good sum of money and land. He says to me, "Fodder, I wouldn't be here if it weren't for you, and to show my appreciation, I want you to have some land. It's good, rich land, with a river runnin' through it, and a mill on it."

Well, I were about as surprised as a fella could be, 'cause I never figured I'd own no land. But I ain't no fool, and Aubrey were a sincere man, so I says, "Thank you, Aubrey," and we shook hands.

Whether or not I saved his life, I ain't too sure of, but when I come up on him at Kettle Hill, he'd been hit in the shoulder and thigh, and he were caught in a bad place with bullets a-whizzin' all around him. I were right strong, so I grabbed him by his good arm and dragged him behind a horse what were dead. Before I charged on up the hill, I told him who I were, and he says to me, "Bless you, Fodder Milo."

I told him to stay low and I'd see to him after we whupped the Spanish. I give him a gun I borrowed off a dead fella and run on up the hill.

I come back after the battle and helped him. He figured I'd saved his life, but I just done somethin' I could do. Weren't nothin' more than that.

Me and Aubrey become good friends, and I checked on him 'til we got back to the United States, and I went to Tennessee. We wrote some letters, and that's how he knowed about Bell and me gittin' married. It were nice of him to come, and his present were a fine thing.

My brother, Denton, and his wife, Lucy, couldn't come to the weddin' but invited us out to Montana to stay a while. And that were our honeymoon.

We rode out on the train and mounted horses what were waitin' for us in Miles City. The trip up the Yellowstone River were a fine one, for sure, and the weather held for us. Nights were clear and full of stars, and we caught us some trout about every day.

Denton had him a place above Billings at the foothills of the Rocky Mountains, and when we got there, him and Lucy said they done worried about us. But we'd just taken our time, 'cause young folks in love don't need to hurry. Bell always talked about them days on the trail and ain't never forgot them. It were just us, and couldn't a-been no better.

Denton had some cattle he messed with, and him and Lucy did a little prospectin' up around Crazy Mountain. Matter of fact, they knowed where some gold were, 'cause a Nez Perce Injun name of Bob White befriended them and told them some secrets about where things were. Denton told me him and Lucy were set, but they lived right simple. Their house were built of logs, and it were real tidy.

We had us a real good time while we were there. Me and Denton fished and prospected, and Lucy made over Bell like she were a little sister.

I got some gold nuggets while I were prospectin', and that come in handy later when I needed money to git my mill runnin'.

Bob White were a real nice Injun, and he took Bell and me to some of the pertiest places I ever seen. He knowed where the best fishin' were, too, but he didn't fish none. He just leaned against a rock and smoked his pipe. When I'd catch a fish, he'd nod a bit and pull out the skillet. That Injun could fix up a meal better than anybody I knowed on the trail. He knowed me and Denton were Buffalo Soldiers, but he liked us anyway, 'cause he says we were like him. I'll never forgit that Injun and his old crumpled dress hat with a eagle feather stuck in it.

After two months, me and Bell said goodbye to Denton and Lucy and come down the Yellowstone. But we had us a guide in old Bob White, and I says to him, "I been hankerin' to see where Custer went under."

So we took a right, up the Big Horn. One day, we come to a hill, and we sat for a while 'til Bob White says, "That's where Yellow Hair felt the strength of the Sioux and Cheyenne."

We were real quiet for a while, just thinkin' about what'd happened. Then Bob says, "The white man called it Custer's last stand, but the red man knows it was his own."

I reckon old Bob White were right in sayin' that.

Bob White left us the next day and went on back to Crazy Mountain. He stayed close to Denton and Lucy 'til they passed on and then went to Canada and trapped varmints 'til he went on to the Happy Huntin' Grounds in 1940.

Me and Bell took our time comin' home, 'cause Montana were a big state. Of course, we were new to each other, so we spent more time than regular folks do, holdin' hands and talkin' about everythin' you can think of. Bell wrote a lot of poetry then, and I were fond of hearin' her recite it to me at night, under that big old Montana sky, all lit up with stars.

Well, when we come home to Tennessee, Bell were with child, and we stayed with the folks 'til after our firstborn come into the world. We named him Shadrock Denton Milo, and he were one fine baby boy.

It weren't long after that, me and Bell and Shad moved to Virginia, where we owned some land and a mill.

Author's journal entry for August 28, 1965

Owls don't talk and say words, but Fodder says they do. I caught a big catfish today, and I bet it weighed twenty pounds. Jarman Clary says that bears live down on the river, but he's just trying to scare me. I'm not afraid of a bear, anyway, because I know a secret about bears that most folks don't know. If I write it, somebody might peek at what I said, and then it won't be a secret, and nobody will be scared of bears. I sat in coon crap today, and I thought Fodder would pass out laughing about it. He played some tunes on his harmonica, and his dog, Buster, started yapping and jumping around. That dog ought to be in a circus, because he's a regular clown.

Brownie Blackmon

Old Brownie Blackmon were one of the finest individuals I ever knowed. When Bell and me come to Virginia, I didn't know a thing about no mill work, but my friend, Aubrey Butler, said he knowed a fella by the name of Brownie Blackmon who'd worked at millin' all his life and might be a-willin' to help.

I were told that Brownie were a little peculiar, but a hard worker. He lived way back in the woods, away from everybody. Didn't have no wife or family. Aubrey give me directions, and one day I set out to find Brownie.

What started out as a perty good trail ended up a footpath. It were a windin' thing, and the forest ain't been timbered in a coon's age. But it were real nice under the trees. When I come to the end of the path, there were a little shack standin' beneath the trees and a fella sittin' on the front step a-whittlin' on a block of wood. I walked up to him and says, "Howdy do!"

He eyeballed me, and without missin' a lick on that wood block, says, "You'd be one Fodda Milo, I reckon."

I told him I were, and what I were up to.

"I'll he'p ya," he said. "But I gotta hunt tomorrey, so's it'll be Wednesd'y a'fo' I'll be dar."

I'd heard he were a big turkey hunter, so I says, "That'll be fine," and I turned to leave.

That's when Brownie opened up and says, "I'm a-whittlin' yo' wife a present, Fodda."

I looked at that block of wood and wondered what it were goin' to be. "She'll like that," I says to him.

He showed a toothless grin and kept on a-whittlin', and I says, "So long!"

On Wednesday, Bell and me were havin' breakfast, when Brownie come a-knockin' on the door. He were nervous and stuttered a little when he seen Bell, but he handed her the pertiest little wood doll I ever seen. Bell just loved it, and I were real surprised that doll come out of a wood block like it done.

Me and Brownie got that mill runnin' in a hurry, and before too long, we had us a good number of customers. I just called it a mill, but everybody else started callin' it Fodder's Mill.

After two years, we were doing so good that I had to take on some workers, and I sold a little land to them to build houses on. It weren't long before we had a little community of folks, and everybody started referrin' to that as Fodder's Mill, too. So I got myself knowed perty good all around, but I didn't holler about it 'cause my mamma always said, "Don't never make ov'a yo'se'f none, 'cause duh Lawd don't like no braggarts!"

I liked workin' the mill, and me and Bell made us a lot of friends. Brownie were my right-hand man at the mill, and when he weren't workin' he were out huntin' turkeys.

One day, he says, "Come on an' go wit' me, Fodda."

So I did.

We were deep in the woods and come on to a big old gang of turkeys, but the forest were real dry, and we couldn't git in close enough for a shot. Brownie figured for a while, then says, "I'm gwine t' run 'round dem birds an' charge in on 'em from duh front. Dey'll scatter ev'awhars, so's ya best be ready fo' a shot at one!" Before he took off, he winked at me and says, "Don't shoot on duh groun', Fodda. Dat's whar I'll be!"

I nodded, and he commenced to runnin' a half circle around them birds, faster than a hound dog.

It weren't long before he come on to that gang of birds head on, and they busted up, wild as could be. I mean to tell you, there were turkeys a-runnin' and a-flyin' everywhere! I shot one comin' over my head, and he dropped at my feet. Then I heard Brownie fire his gun, and when we found each other, we both had us a turkey in hand and a smile across our faces. Yep, Brownie Blackmon were the best turkey hunter I ever did see. He were a true friend, too, and them is hard to find. Brownie'd stick with you through hard times.

I recollect once when the owner of another mill got hisself jealous that I were doin' so good, I got me a visit from Aubrey Butler. Aubrey says to me, "Fodder, Bill Jackson's a Klansman, and he's in with a nasty bunch from North Carolina." Aubrey were a good friend to warn me, and he said that he'd do what he could.

Well, everybody got real scared about it all, so I called a meetin' of my workers, and everybody in the community of Fodder's Mill showed up. Ned Harris found out when the Klan were comin', and I struck on a plan.

It weren't long after that, that me and Brownie were closin' up one evenin', and down the road come about a dozen Klansmen all decked out in sheets and hoods and carryin' torches. They were ridin' horses and drew them up around the front door where me and Brownie were standin'. Brownie were smokin' his pipe, like usual, and I were about to light up when one of them spoke up and says, "We come to shut down yo' mill, boy!"

Now, when a man insults you, it's best to toss it around in your mind for a minute and figure where it come from. Most times it's goin' to come out of his lack of somethin', and if he says it loud so everybody can hear, it'll be some struttin' involved.

I figured this were a case of both, so I says this to him. "My name's Fodder Milo, and I ain't got no fear of the likes of none of you. I done hunted bears and wildcats what smelled better than the likes of you. I done fought Injuns and Spanish who had more courage in their dyin' hearts than all of you put together, a-hidin' under your bed sheets! The likes of you killed my cousin, Fiddle Moody, for nothin', and I ain't forgot it, neither. So you best turn and skedaddle while you can!"

Bill Jackson were fidgety under his bed sheet, and he put his hand on his gun and says, "Boys, let's burn the mill down!"

But when I struck a match to light my pipe, you could hear the guns cockin' behind the trees and bushes, and them Klansmen got real quiet and nervous.

Brownie spoke then and says, "Don't nobody gots to know 'bout dis, Mista Jackson, if'n ya jest ride off. But if'n ya don't, fo'ks'll always wonder whatev'a happened to ya."

I didn't say no more, and about that time, Aubrey Butler and some fellas I knowed come ridin' up and seen there were trouble.

Aubrey told everybody to calm down, and then he spoke to Bill Jackson in private. I don't know what he said, but the Klan rode off, and I never

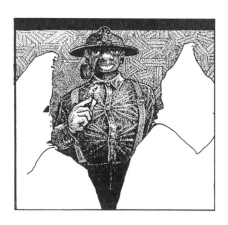

had no more trouble from them.

Later, Aubrey asked me if I'd a-killed them, and I thanked him for showin' up when he did. I also thanked Brownie for stickin' with me. Lord knows there were better things to do that day.

Brownie died with a bad heart in 1928, and me and Bell and the children were real sad, 'cause he were like a member of the family for a long time. In all the years I knowed him, he were nothin' but good and honest.

I'll tell you a funny story about him what happened a year or two before he passed on.

Now, Brownie were brave and weren't scared of much, but he believed in haints, and that were enough to git a laugh on him.

There were a fella name of Shuck Jones, who stuttered right bad, and he were a huntin' buddy of Brownie's. Shuck were right old and weren't able to do no hard work, so he'd pick up a job trimmin' hedges or sittin' with tobacco fires so they wouldn't git out of hand and burn down nobody's barn. It were easy work, and if Shuck were sittin' with a fire near Brownie's place, then they'd visit a little. Brownie'd come walkin' up in the dark, and old Shuck'd say, "Wh-who-who-uh you?"

Brownie'd say who he were, and they'd sit and smoke pipes and yap about huntin' turkeys.

Well, one night, old Shuck were sittin' outside the barn door of Wink Powell's place and must've died in his sleep. He'd done leaned back against the wall with his pipe in his hand, when Brownie walked up out of the woods. It were dark, and Brownie could barely see Shuck sittin' there like usual. But he didn't know Shuck done passed on yet.

Well, a hoot owl must've lit on the barn door, 'cause when Brownie said, "Howdy do, Shuck," he heard Shuck say back, "Wh-who-who-uh you?"

Brownie says, "It's me, Brownie."

But instead of Shuck sayin', "Howdy do, Brownie," he says again, "Wh-who-who-uh you?"

Well, Brownie figured somethin' weren't right, so he come right up to Shuck and lit a match, and about the time he seen Shuck's dead face, that owl says, "Wh-who-who-uh you?" and commenced to flappin' its wings right over Brownie's head. In a split second, Brownie decided old Shuck done turned into a haint, and he would've took off like a wild buck, but his feet got tangled up on Shuck's cane, and he fell flat on his face. That weren't so bad, 'cept that all the commotion caused Shuck's body to fall over, and he landed on Brownie's back, and Brownie knowed he were a goner, for sure, then. He let out a holler and rolled out from under old Shuck, and he broke a trail back through them pine woods what couldn't be made no better if he'd cut it with a axe.

I never figured why Brownie didn't die that night. His heart were gittin' bad by then. But I'm glad he stayed on, 'cause I sure did have a time ribbin' him about bein' hainted by Shuck Jones. He never admitted it were a owl what talked to him that night, but that's all right, 'cause that's the way Brownie were.

Author's journal entry for September 8, 1965

I caught four bass and two bream the other day at the river, and Fodder caught three bream and a catfish. He smoked a pipe the whole time, and I told him I want to smoke a pipe, but he said it will stunt my growth. I like his clothes. He wears the same ones all the time, but he doesn't stink, because he washes his clothes every two days. I wish I could wear the same clothes every day. Sometimes I don't wear anything when I'm alone in the wild woods. I just stick my clothes in a hole in a tree and cut me a spear and hunt like the Indians did. I have a call I do sometimes, but it's not as good as Tarzan's. One time I did it real loud when Fodder was fishing, and he didn't know I was in the woods. He looked around but couldn't see me. He said he thought something bad was in the woods, but I told him it was just me, and he asked me to do it again. When I did, his eyes got real big, and he asked me if my mamma knew she'd given birth to a wild animal. He was just teasing, so I told him I got a "pug" mark on my birth certificate. But you can't fool Fodder Milo.

Boler and the Butterfly

One day, Bell and me were sittin' at the kitchen table when our youngest boy, Boler, come bustin' through the front door like he were late for a fire and talkin' some jibberish about a big butterfly done changed into a angel.

I says, "Boy, don't be talkin' no foolishness."

And Bell smiles and says, "Come here, Boler, and tell your mamma what ya saw."

I just looked over at that woman and winked, and she give me a scold with her eyes 'cause she don't think nothin' of nobody puttin' down a young un's imagination. So I just chuckled and watched that boy over my readin' specks.

There weren't nothin' sly about Boler, and he were convicted to his words like a preacher to the pulpit. Said he'd been down at the river and weren't catchin' nothin' when he heard a ringin' in his ears, and his heart got to flutterin', and he heard a voice like his granny's say, "Come along, chil', an' folla me." But when Boler looked around, he didn't see nobody. So he shut his eyes real tight and commenced to prayin' hard. Then he heard that voice again say, "Open yo' eyes, chil', an' folla me to duh garden."

When the boy opened his eyes, he seen this butterfly flutterin' over his head. He held out his hand, and the thing lit on his finger, and it weren't like no butterfly he'd ever seen. So he says, "You is a mighty perty thing." Then he remembered me tellin' him when he were just a little fella that the butterflies is God's messengers, spreadin' love and givin' us beauty amidst our struggles. I ain't seen no harm in describin' somethin' so perty in such a way. So I let it stand, and I ain't guilty in my heart at all for it.

When Boler spoke to the butterfly, it fluttered up and around and headed up to the house, and he took off after it. Shad were off in the woods at the time. The baby were playin' in the yard when the thing lit on her head and then fluttered around her face, causing her to laugh and get up to follow it. So Anna and Boler chased that butterfly to the flower garden behind the house, and the ringin' come back to the boy. They were lookin' for the butterfly, when Boler heard Anna say, "Granny," and he looked up and seen a angel driftin' over the tulips. She were dressed in a long gown, and the sun were shinin' right through her.

Boler said he weren't afraid, 'cause it looked like his granny. But she were young and didn't have no bent back or pain in her face, so he took his sister by the hand and walked up to the angel.

She touched them on their heads and smiled real nice. Then she commenced to fadin' away, and that's when Boler come runnin' in to fetch me and Bell. We come out and didn't see nothin' in the garden. But little Anna said she were with her granny out there.

I walked over to Miz Trudy's house after lunch that day to give her a pie Bell made for her, but she done passed on. Found her lyin' in bed, just like she were sleepin'. Had a old photograph in her hand of Bell and the children standin' in the tulips. I reckon she needed to see them one more time before she went on.

I don't doubt it none, 'cause you cain't explain everything. Sometimes I git to thinkin' about what Boler told us, but it don't fret me none. I know a child can see things us old folks is blind to. That seems natural enough, I suppose.

Author's journal entry for September 13, 1965

I wish I had a coon dog. There are a lot of coons on the river. If I caught one, I'd make me a coonskin hat like Davy Crockett. Mandy brought me a salted rabbit skin, but it started to stink, so I threw it away. Fodder says a coon is kin to a bear, and you should never corner one or it'll tear into you. I got a 410 shotgun to hunt with. Fodder doesn't hunt anymore. He just fishes, but he says if I shoot him a squirrel or two this winter, he'll show me how to fix them up. Fodder Milo is a good man to spend time with, and he's always happy to see me coming. If he's not down at the river, I go to his house. I know the trail to his house real good. Sometimes we just sit on the porch and listen to the birds in the woods. I like him to tell me stories. That's the best thing for me. And I like horehound candy. Fodder always has a bag of horehound candy in his pocket, just like my Grandpa Clabo. It will cure some things. At least, that's what both of them say.

Shad and the Coon Dog

Our oldest boy, Shad, were a huntin' trick when he were young. He'd be off in the woods about every day, but I didn't stop him from doin' that, 'cause it ain't right to put a harness on a young 'un's spirit. Besides, he were always puttin' rabbit and squirrel on the table, and I were partial to them both.

One day, Shad come home with the poorest lookin' hound dog I ever seen, and he says, "Kin I have 'im, Papa?"

I figured it wouldn't hurt nobody for him to have a hound dog, so I says, "Sure!"

It weren't but a few weeks before that boy had Bull Run (that's the name he give him) filled out and perky as a hound can git.

One evenin' he says to me, "Will ya come coonin' wit' me an' Bull Run tonight, Papa?"

And I says, "Sure!" even though it were somethin' I ain't never done before.

So, after supper, we got the gun, a lantern, and a axe and went lookin' for a coon. I ain't got nothin' against coons, but I wouldn't eat one if it were the last varmint on earth and my life depended on it. But a coon do have a perty coat, and that were enough for me to be all right with killin' one, 'cause my papa always said, "If'n ya ain't gonna eat it or wear it, den don't go a-killin' it."

We walked down on the river bank, and Bull Run got him a whiff of coon. Shad let him off the rope, and that hound committed hisself to a chase what had us up and down the ridges. It were right fun to start with, but after I got slapped in the face a few times by tree limbs and such, it were about to become a chore. I were gittin' out of breath when, all of a sudden, Bull Run must've treed that coon, 'cause he stopped howlin' and commenced to whinin' and barkin'.

Shad says, "He's down on duh riv'a bank, ag'in."

And we hurried on down.

Now, I seen a lot of things in my life, but what Bull Run done were it, for sure! We seen where he

run down the hill and into the hollow of a big fat sycamore tree what done leaned out over the river. I figured that coon done run into the hollow of that tree and come out a knothole somewhere. But that weren't the problem.

The problem were that Bull Run done gone in after him and weren't able to git nothin' through that knothole 'cept his fool head. And that's where he were—just as stuck as you can git. And to make it worse, the coon knowed he were helpless and were a-hissin' and a-slappin' at his nose. Bull Run done got hisself in a fix, for sure!

Shad says to me, "What we gwine t' do?"

I cut a branch and took the lantern and walked out on that tree, where I beat that coon off Bull Run. The coon fell in the water and swum off. So I reached up into the hollow of that tree and pulled at Bull Run's hind legs. But he were stuck good. I had to be careful not to fall off that tree, 'cause I weren't no boy no more, and it were about all I could do to git back to the river bank without takin' a swim. I says to Shad, "I ain't never seen no dog do nothin' like this before now."

Shad stayed there while I went to the house to git some lard what to grease Bull Run's head and neck with.

We worked on that dog for a long time before he come loose, and then about soon as he got his feet on the river bank, he were off a-howlin' again. I says to Shad, "I done had enough, Son."

And he says back, "Kin I foller 'im, Papa?"

I says, "You best do, 'cause he's the wildest thing about a coon I ever seen."

I were one tired man when I got home.

And with a smile on her face, Bell says, "How'd ya like coon huntin', Fodda?"

"Shad can have it," I told her. And I ain't took a notion to go coon huntin' no more.

Shad and Bull Run went coonin' a lot after that. But, one night, that fool hound run into somethin' what stopped him cold, and we never seen him again.

Author's journal entry for October 7, 1965

Fodder can smell a storm coming. He smelled one today, and we got to his house just before it started to rain. I was cold, so he gave me some hot tea and cornbread. I sat in a big rocking chair, and he told me a story about the apple orchard in the meadow through the woods. His wife died a few years ago, and his children are grownups. They don't live around here, so he don't see them much. I wish I could live with Fodder, because he's my good friend and tells the best stories. We talked about ghosts today. He calls them "haints," but they don't scare him. He says a haint is just a spirit that hasn't found its way yet. I believe that. Sometimes I feel things I can't explain. It's like you're not alone, but you are by yourself. I think sometimes Indian spirits come around me when I'm in the wild woods. They know I got their blood in me because I'm a roaming boy that's half wild.

Jasmin's Apple Tree

Losin' a child is a hard thing on folks. Me and Bell lost a baby girl we named Jasmin. She were Anna's twin, and come into the world about ten minutes before Anna.

They were the pertiest little angels I ever seen, but about a week after they were born, Jasmin got to ailin', and two weeks later the Lord took her back. Old Doc Ruby said her little system weren't strong enough to handle the world outside her mamma.

Jasmin died in Bell's arms, and weren't a thing I could do 'cept be there. It were about the saddest day of our lives.

Me and Brownie dug a grave beneath the apple tree what stood alone down in the meadow. Bell could see that tree from the house, and she said it'd be a nice place for Jasmin to sleep. That were the spring of 1910, and that apple tree were bloomin' real perty. It were a heart-broke set of folks who come under that tree to say goodbye to Jasmin. The Lord give us a perty day for it.

I don't think Bell ever got herself over the loss of that baby. That's why she always made such a fuss over Anna.

Now, Anna were a handful, all right. She were always into somethin' and had a imagination like I ain't never seen. She'd come up with the sweetest little rhymes and were always full of fun. I'd sit her on my knee, and we'd try to out-rhyme each other about silly things.

Bell made all Anna's clothes, and to see that child dressed in her Sunday best were always a joy to me. She were perty as a flower.

In the spring when that apple tree commenced to bloomin', Anna'd pick a blossom off it every day and wear it, 'cause she knowed her sister were sleepin' under that tree, and somewhere along the way, her mamma done said to her that Jasmin were perty as a apple blossom.

Anna spent a lot of time playin' down at that tree. She'd climb it and swing on its limbs. Sometimes she'd just run around it like somebody were chasin' her or somethin'. And she were always talkin' and singin' down there. Bell'd hear her and tell me sometimes, "Fodda, I'm worried that Anna's alone too much."

But I never thought that child were lonely, 'cause she were a happy thing.

One day when Anna were five year old, she come down with somethin' what made her real weak. I figured she had a bug, 'til over a week done passed and she weren't no better. Doc Ruby took a look at her and says she weren't digestin' her food right, and he give us a list of things she could eat, and some medicine. She got worse and finally wouldn't eat nothin' for nobody. I couldn't git her to drink nothin' 'cept a little sugar water. We were gittin' real scared and decided on takin' her to the hospital in Richmond. But the night before we were goin' to leave, somethin' happened what turned my way of thinkin' about some things.

It were a full-moon night, and I were sleepin' when Bell touched me and says, "Fodda, Anna's down at the apple tree."

Well, I looked out the window, and she sure were. I couldn't believe it, 'cause she were so weak she couldn't hardly git up out the bed. But there she were, sittin' in that tree in her nightgown and just a-singin' so sweet.

Bell and me went down there, and she quieted her singin' and says to us, "I needs to eat three apples from Jasmin's tree every day, and I'll git well."

Bell says, "Who told you that, girl?"

Anna whispered to us, "Dar's a voice in duh tree what talks to me an' sings me duh nicest songs."

It were a little chilly, so I reached up and took Anna down from the tree and says to her, "Sure it do, honey."

When we got that child back into bed, we talked for a while, 'til I fell on back to sleep. But Bell didn't sleep none.

Next mornin' I found her in the kitchen with about a bushel of apples she'd done picked from that apple tree.

"We're not goin' to Richmond t'day, Fodda," she says.

"You goin' to give Anna apples off that tree, ain't you, Bell?"

And she says, "Yes, I am."

I went into Anna's room, and she smiled at me and looked up with them big chocolate eyes and says, "Ya believes me, don't ya, Papa?"

"What did the voice say to you, Anna?"

And she told me it wanted her to eat nothin' but apples off it, and drink water for three days. I figured it wouldn't hurt her none, so I says, "'Course I believe you, honey."

Then she told me the voice wanted Bell to save the apple seeds 'til she had a bucket full.

When I told Bell that, she wanted to know why. But all Anna done told me were her mamma'd know why later.

Well, don't you know that from that day on, Anna commenced to gittin' her strength back, and by the third day, she were up and perky as ever. Doc Ruby come by and couldn't figure it. But he took home some of them apples.

Bell'd pick them apples every other day 'til they were all gone, and we ate them cooked and peeled and mashed, and nary a seed were lost. Bell had her bucket of seeds just like Anna said. She didn't have no idea what to do with them 'til, one night, a little voice come to her in a dream and says, "Plant the seeds in the meadow."

Well, we done it! In a few years we had us a orchard, and it were sure perty in the spring when them trees bloomed. It looked like the meadow were covered in snow. We had us so many apples that Aubrey Butler told us we ought to sell them. So we did! And before long, we were sendin' Jasmin apples all over the country. Had to hire us some folks to help with the pickin'.

Bell and Anna saw to most of the business, 'cause I were busy with the mill 'til I retired in 1936. Then it were Jasmin apples what were the family business for another ten year.

Sometimes I wonder when I think about it all comin' from Anna bein' sick. Brownie said she'd done heard her sister. But I don't know for sure. Maybe it were Jasmin. Maybe trees can talk to you, if you know how to hear them. I ain't never done it yet, but sometimes I think I hear things when I'm real quiet.

When Jasmin's tree died in 1944, Bell had me to make her a rockin' chair with the wood from it. She sure did love that rockin' chair. I told Anna she could have it someday. But I sit and rock in it now, 'cause it's a fine chair, and it were Bell's.

I sure miss my Bell.

Author's journal entry for June 12, 1966

J. B. Reid says he's going to strike me out this summer in baseball, but I don't think so. He hasn't yet. He's a real good pitcher and throws sidearm and fast. A lot of the boys on the team are afraid of him. That's why they strike out. But I just grin at him and smack whatever he throws. We have a good time kidding about it. I play for the V. F. W. Indians. I wish J. B. played on my team. We need a good pitcher like him. I visited Billy Peebles yesterday. He's a good friend of mine. One day at school, a black girl named Gracy Jackson leaned too far over her desk and fell on the floor. She couldn't get up, and nobody would help her. Billy got up and helped her and picked up her books. She was crying because I think she was hurt a little. Some boys called Billy names and were talking about beating him up outside. But I told them not to touch him because he did the right thing, and he was the only one that did and I had respect for him. Nobody hurt Billy, and that's good, because he didn't see color that day. He just saw somebody that needed help. I think Billy is going to be a good man one day.

A Boy Named Michael

In the early spring of 1935, Bell and me took us a little trip down to Atlanta to see a cousin of Bell's who weren't gettin' along so good. Sally Wintree were her name, and she done lost her man in the war and been livin' with her mamma for a long time.

The Ford I were drivin' at the time weren't too reliable, so Bell and me took the train. Now, if you got some thinkin' to do or you're one that likes to read books, then a train ride is a good thing. You sure ain't goin' to git no sleep on one, though, unless you're just bone tired.

Well, I were right well-rested, and Bell said I ought to sit next to the window 'cause she had a book or two to pass the time with, and I were fond of seein' out the window on a train ride. Besides, I didn't read much then. It were hard for me to know the big words, since I never did git much learnin'. But it were a long way down to Georgia, and after a while, my eyes got tired from watchin' out the window, and I asked Bell what she were readin'.

She showed me the front of her book and says to me, "I'm readin' the essays of Henry David Thoreau."

She don't talk like me' 'cause she done went to school when she were young, and she always spoke just right and knew all the words in the books she read. That woman were always readin' and were a happy thing when she'd git her hands on a new book of the day. She read all the classics, and that's how I come to know some of what I know about them, 'cause Bell were a fine storyteller, and she'd tell me stories she said I ought to know. 'Cause of that woman, I know the stories of Moby Dick and Rumpelstiltskin and Gulliver's Travels. She got me to readin', too. But, sometimes, I'd skip over the big words I weren't able to say, unless she were around, and then Bell would help me say them. She were good at that and never did make me feel bad about my lack of schoolin'. It were just between us.

Bell showed me a photograph of the man who wrote the essays she were readin', and I noticed he were a white man with a beard, and eyes that made me think he could know you just by lookin' at you. Bell said he were cut different from most men of his day and weren't afraid to say his mind and stand by it. She said she'd finished readin' the book and were about to commence a new one. So I said I'd have a go at it, and she give me the book.

Well, I had a little trouble gittin' it all, but by the time we pulled into the station in Atlanta, I'd done finished two of that man's writin's, and I were real impressed with him and what all he said. Here were a white man who had stood against slavery and even went to jail before he'd let the government force him to do somethin' against his spirit. I found myself likin' Henry David Thoreau, and I remembered some of what I read that day.

When we got to Atlanta, it were loud and bustlin', and we found Sally in a terrible way. So, Bell commenced to doctorin' her and cookin' for the family, and I did all I could do to help.

One day, Bell says to me, "Fodda, you've been such a help an' all, but you haven't seen much of the city. Why don't you get on, now?"

So I got my chores done and walked over to the city, and it were one busy place, for sure! There were cars and trucks and buses everywhere, and more folks than you could shake a stick at. I went in some stores and bought me a bag of horehound candy, 'cause I done run out of it and been lovin' it all my life. I got to feelin' hungry after a while and got me a soda and some corn pone on the street, and it were real good.

On the way back to the house that day, I seen a little boy sittin' by hisself on a grassy hill. Now, I might not a-paid no attention to that boy, except that there were butterflies flutterin' over his head. Now, he didn't have no idea, 'cause his face were in his hands, and he were lookin' down at the ground. I were drawn to that little boy, so I crossed the street and walked up to him and said, "Hey there, little boy, you got butterflies over your head."

When he looked up at me, there were tears

rollin' down his face, and he commenced to wipin' them away so I wouldn't see them.

"What's the matter, son, you hurt or somethin'?"

He shook his head.

It were then that a little white butterfly lit on the end of my nose, and I reckon when I opened my eyes wide to see what it were, I must've looked silly or somethin', 'cause that sad little boy smiled and said, "He gonna fly up yo' nose, Mista."

Well, I waved that butterfly off my nose and laughed, too.

"What's yo' name, Mista?"

And I says, "Fodder Milo." I tipped my hat and sat down on the grass next to him. "What done fretted you, son?" I asked.

But he didn't want to say, so I didn't ask no more, but I seen he were lookin' down the road at some white children who were swingin' on some board swings in a little park. I figured somethin' done happened with them, but I weren't goin' to bring it up, so, instead, I says, "What's your name, son?"

"Michael," he says.

"Well, now, that's a good name." I dipped into my coat pocket and brung out that bag of horehound candy. I took me a piece and held the bag open for my new little friend.

He reached over and peeked in the bag, then poked his hand in and got him a piece. Soon as he popped it in his mouth, he smiled and says to me,

"Thank ya, Mista Milo."

And I says back, "Fodder, son. Just, Fodder."

He looked at me kind of funny, then asked, "Where'd ya git a name like dat?"

And I says, "My papa give it to me, son, 'cause I reckon he liked the sound of it."

The little boy shrugged his shoulders.

I says, "Besides, a name's somethin' you ain't got much to say about."

"Do you like it, Fodda Milo?"

And I says to him, "Folks don't usually forgit it."

That boy smiled and says, "My daddy's gonna change his name, an' mine."

"Well, if it makes you both happy, son," I says, "then that's all right. But Michael's a good name."

We got to talkin' for a while, and, finally, he tells me that he were swingin' on the swings with them white boys when one of their daddy's come out and told him to git on, 'cause that weren't no place for colored folks. I knowed that hurt the boy, what with him being so young and all. But I told him that maybe one day that would change, and he asked me if I really thought so. That's when I told him about what I'd read on the train.

That boy seemed real impressed that a white man would write such things. I told him one day he's goin' to read the writin's of Henry David Thoreau, and that he weren't the only white man that knowed that things weren't right.

After a while that boy says, "It's two worlds, Fodda Milo, one fo' dem, an' one fo' us." He were lookin' down the road.

I says to him, "But it's one government, son, and governments change, 'cause of the people who run them. The black man been searchin' for his place for a long time, now, and he's felt the weight of the chains what bound him in the past. But he ain't shackled no more, and when the pride of freedom takes him over inside, then self-respect will lift him up. If the laws is wrong, then the law got to be changed. But the laws won't set a man free, son. It's the man what sets the laws free. Mista Thoreau said, 'The character inherent in the American people has done all that's been accomplished.' We got to let go of the past. There ain't no more chains. Just them what's inside us. Right is right, and wrong is wrong. There ain't no middle ground. Not when it comes to the rights of the people. It don't matter what color your skin is."

Well, I went on 'til I stopped with it, and to tell the truth, I surprised myself a little, 'cause I ain't never said so much on the spur of the minute like that. But I think that little boy understood what I were sayin'.

Once I stopped talkin' he were quiet for a minute, and then he says to me, "Fodda Milo, ya ought'a write yo' own book."

And I chuckled and says, "No, son, you just read Thoreau, 'cause he got a way with words, and I ain't got the learnin' to write no book."

Then I looked at my watch and seen it were time to git on.

That little boy stood up and shook my hand and says, "I'll read dem writin's o' dat man one day, Fodda Milo."

And I left him there on the grassy hill, thinkin' he were all right.

Bell's Cousin Sally got well enough for us to leave after about two weeks, and we took the train back home.

Time went on, and, one day some years ago, I were visitin' relatives in Montgomery, Alabama, when I seen this man in the pulpit who got to quotin' Henry David Thoreau. I enjoyed his sermon, and the folks in the congregation were feelin' the spirit that day. After the service, I found that preacher and shook his hand, and I says to him, "I remember a little boy named 'Michael' who had butterflies around his head and tears on his face."

Well, he about passed out when he heard that, and he hugged me and says, "I remember you, Fodda Milo." He had tears in his eyes when he recalled that day, and he told me he'd read them writin's. But I knowed he had by what he'd said in the pulpit. We had us a good visit that day, and then I left.

Now, I hear his name on the radio and see it

in the paper all the time. He's doin' what the Lord called him to do. And I ain't surprised, 'cause even when he were little, he were all right. Sometimes folks act like they don't believe me when I says I knowed Martin Luther King, Jr., when he were just a little boy. So I don't say it much. But every time I hear his name or see a picture of him, I remember that day down in Georgia. Seems like it were just yesterday.

Author's journal entry for July 8, 1966

Today, on my way to the river, I saw an albino deer. I think it was a buck, but it didn't have any antlers. He scared me a little when I first saw him because I've never seen anything that big and white in the woods before. We just stood there and looked at each other for a minute, and then he walked away. I wonder what he thought of me. You don't shoot an albino deer. My grandma says they are a special creature from God, and man doesn't have the right to kill things of such beauty. I think God wanted me to see that deer, so I will have a good memory when I get old. I told Fodder about it, and he said that my grandma is right about them. Fodder and I see a lot of deer down on the Meherrin River. I think the woods are like a city to the animals when we're not around to scare them off. I have a dog named Dutchess. She's a Spitz that my folks got when my sister was born. I don't like the name Dutchess, so I call her Dutch or Dutchie. She's real smart, and fast, too. Sometimes when we've been away for a while and come home, she'll get so excited that she'll bark and run circles around the house. We got some rabbit beagles, too. My favorite one is named Hassaway. My Uncle Armalee gave her to us, and I don't think there's ever been a better rabbit dog. She doesn't run deer, either. I'm going to write a story about her one day.

Buster and Me

It don't seem too long ago that Buster come to live here with me and Bell. He were give to us by a friend, and I reckon he were about the best gift we could git. He ain't never cost me a penny, 'cause he hunts a little and mostly eats scraps from the table. That dog'll eat greens if they got just a little pork fat in them, and no vinegar. I seen him eat apples, too, and there ain't a lot of dogs around what'll swallow up a apple.

Bell said he weren't nothin' but a perty old possum, with a appetite big as a hog's. But she sure did think a lot of that dog. She didn't like for me to feed him at the table, but then, sometimes when she didn't think I were lookin', she'd slip a little somethin' to him. So I just didn't say nothin' about that, and it went on that way right up to the day she passed on.

Buster missed that woman somethin' awful when she went to be with the Lord. He used to lay by her rockin' chair in the evenin' when she were readin' or writin'. And sometimes he'd just stay at the house with her instead of goin' off fishin' with me. But when that woman went on, he wouldn't ever leave my side. Best friend I ever had besides

Bell. She would tell me what were right sometimes, but old Buster just goes along with whatever I say, and he ain't never said nothin' what would make me think he weren't in agreement with me all the way. He's a funny dog, the way he skips around and yelps when I play the harmonica.

But the funniest thing I ever seen were once when he were still young and we were walkin' across the field, a big old buck deer come runnin' out the woods. He were a mighty animal, for sure, and he were kickin' up his hoofs and makin' tracks across that field, when Buster seen him and took out after him.

Well, Buster were a-rantin' at the top of his

lungs, and givin' chase with all he had, and the two of them went on over the hill, into the woods where I couldn't see them no more. But I could hear that dog just a-howlin', 'til, all of a sudden, I heard him yelp right good. It weren't long 'til he come a-runnin' over the hill, fast as he could, and that big buck deer were right behind him! I ain't never seen nothin' like it in all my days!

Well, I got to laughin' at that dog, 'cause he sure were a pitiful sight, a-runnin' for his life like he were doin'. I believe that buck deer would've run him down, too, if I hadn't waved my hands and shouted off like I done. It were all I could do to calm that dog down after that, and he shook the rest of the day.

Buster'll hunt up a varmint now and then, but I ain't never seen him give chase to no buck deer no more after that day. I don't blame him none, but sometimes I laugh about it to myself.

Author's journal entry for August 2, 1966

I wrote a little story yesterday and read it to Fodder. It's called "Journey to a Rainbow," and it's about a place in the big woods across a wide river where people are good and peaceful. There's a big rainbow that is always over this place, but it's hard to get there, and the path is full of danger. I like the wild woods because it's peaceful for me. Mamma says I have to talk up more to people and get more friends, but I got enough friends, and I don't like to talk a lot when nobody is really saying anything. I listen more than I talk, and that way I learn more. Fodder says it's not bad to be quiet. Last week we walked up into the pine woods and sat down and listened to the doves cooing. I'll bet there were a hundred or more in the trees. It was peaceful, and we didn't say anything for a long time. Buster and me fell asleep, and Fodder just let us alone until we woke up. On the way back to Fodder's house, he told me a funny story about a catfish he caught one time. He showed me the hole where he caught it, too.

Choice

We're all, in some ways, creatures of habit. That's right, and if you don't believe it, then just take a peek at yourself.

You come alive in the mornin' and git hungry real quick. And once you're filled up and your belly ain't naggin' you, there's chores to do. Same chores every day, rain or shine. And if you're lucky enough to have yourself a job, then it ain't no difference, 'cause a job's the same, day in and day out. Same faces, same names. Same, same, same! It can be a bore, except for one thing, and that's choice. C-H-O-I-C-E. Choice! That's the only thing what breaks the routine of your life. It lifts you up or drives you down.

I knowed a man once who had a good wife, respectful children, and enough money to live good. I reckon life become a bore to him, 'cause somewhere along in his mid-years, he figured his wife weren't so fine no more, so he took to gallivantin'. I also suspect he got fed up with his financial security, so he commenced to gamblin' 'til he lost all he had. That man's wife left him and took his children, who weren't so respectful of him no more, since they found out about his gallivantin'.

And one day that once-happy man went and sent hisself a-knockin' on heaven's door. He were alone and poorer than a snake in a barrel.

At his funeral I heard a old lady say, "He used to have a good life, 'til he went bad. Wonder why?"

And a bug-eyed gentleman in a gray suit says, "I don't know why he ended up dis way!"

I didn't say nary a word when the Reverend were goin' on about his chances of gainin' entry into the Pearly Gates, but I knowed without bein' poked too hard that everything that come his way were by choice. Didn't nobody tell him to gallivant or gamble. And nobody put that gun to his head, neither. He just plain long exercised his freedom of choice. And the grave digger and the undertaker reaped the outcome. Could've been different, but men ain't bent the same, and what rules them is as mysterious as 'tis common.

Now, fish ain't much different. I knowed a fish I called Mista Spud Green, what claimed a hole down by the gaugin' station. He wouldn't let no other fish in his hole, and if one come around what were small enough, old Spud'd scoff him up right quick. I seen him chase off big fish, then come back to the same place, like it were his castle or somethin'.

I tried to catch Spud sometimes, but he'd act like he knowed what I were up to and let hisself sink on down, out of sight, then come back up when I says, "Shucks," or somethin' like that.

I don't reckon a fish in its natural habitat is goin' to live too long, since somethin's always lookin' to eat it. So I set my sights on makin' old Spud Green my dinner before he might slide down the goozle of a creature less deservin' than myself.

I commenced a rigorous regimen of offerin' bait to that fat old catfish every day at seven in the mornin' and at noon.

Well, it weren't long before I got a little bewildered. Come to find out, Mista Spud Green were as ornery about his choice of meals as he were about guests around his place. I brung him everything I could fit on a hook, if it smelled bad enough and looked half as good. He'd just mosey up to it and kind of blow it away like it weren't good enough for him. That would befuddle me, 'til I'd git sort of outdone and say somethin' what Bell might've got after me for. But I did git outdone with Mista Spud Green like that for a while, 'til, one night, I got to thinkin' about choice. Old Spud didn't git big as he were by starvin' hisself, and a catfish'll eat just about anything if it's nasty enough or causes him grief. So I figured he had a fix on me and reckoned it to his best interest not to bite nothin' when I were around.

I says to him one mornin', "You think you know me, Mista Spud Green, but old Fodder ain't so simple as to let a fish have at him." Then I fell upon a plan.

I didn't visit Spud for a few days, and when I'd come by the gaugin' station, I'd walk out of my way so he couldn't see me. One day, I got weak and snuck around, hidin' myself behind a fat sycamore and dropped a line for a while. Had a gob of worms on that hook just a-wigglin' and all. But Spud just blew at them and sunk on down. I think he seen me, and that made me feel a little foolish, to fret about what a fish might think of me, so I slunk away, but I says real quiet-like, "I'll be back, you old rascal, 'cause I got a plan what will git you in my fryin' pan, for sure!"

About four days after that, it were hot, and the skeetas weren't lettin' man or beast go unfettered. I set my mind to thinkin' that this were *the* day! So when the evenin' come, I took a rotten chicken liver and a can of night crawlers, two poles and my fly rod and made my way to the gaugin' station. Old Buster come along that day and were trottin' through the weeds, jumpin' up the grasshoppers. One big brown one lit on my shirt pocket, and I poked him down in there with a smile on my face, 'cause I were thinkin' about that catfish, Mista Spud Green, and how he ain't seen me lately.

Now when I come to the gaugin' station, I says to Buster, "You best keep hushed now, dog, and sit!"

And he done just like that, 'cause he do what I say most of the time.

I commenced to decoratin' one big hook with that chicken liver, and it smelled somethin' fierce, so when I finished, I rubbed dirt on my hands to git off the stench. Then I hung a gob of night crawlers on another hook, like I ain't never done before, and give a spit of tobacco juice on them so they'd sting a little and wiggle right good.

When I'd finished baitin' the hooks just right, I commenced to sneak up to that fat sycamore tree and git up close, so I could git me a look at Spud's hole. But he weren't goin' to show hisself, and I didn't mind, 'cause I knowed that he were down deep and out of sight. I reached them two cane poles out and got them hooks set, one a little deeper than the other. I didn't use no regular corks on them, neither, but ones I whittled from a wine cork. Spud knowed my others too good. Knowin' how he were about takin' bait, it didn't fret me none not to sit there and watch for him. I backed away real quiet and told Buster, "Now, you best stay," and he just laid there, with his head on his paws, like he knowed I were up to somethin'.

I got my fly rod and hurried downstream to a shallow place where the deer cross, and I walked on over to the other side of the river. Got my feet and pants wet, but I didn't fret, 'cause I were busy and thinkin' one thing.

When I come opposite the gaugin' station, I stayed low and come up to where a old tree trunk hid me from Spud's sight. It were then I collected that big brown and yellow grasshopper from my shirt pocket and hooked him at the tip of his tail with my fly hook. I says to him, "Do what you got to do," and he tried to git away, but I had him and tossed him into Spud's hole.

Well, about two blinks later, there's a swell in the water, and you'd a-thought Jonah's whale done broke the surface. I let him take it a little before I yanked hard and set the hook. Then I knowed, for sure, I were fightin' Mista Spud Green! He commenced to headin' to the bottom, and went back and forth. Sometimes he'd come almost to the top, then I'd see a fin, and he'd head back down again.

Now, don't you think I were goin' to land that old catfish with a fly rod, lest I were willin' to let him tire hisself out first. So I set my mind to just that. I sat on that tree trunk and spoke to him like I would a worthy opponent. I says, "Now you been snagged by one Fodder Milo, you old rascal! And I intend to bring you to my fryin' pan!"

I kept that line taut but let him do the work, and after a good while, he give up, and I brung him onto the sand.

Well, if I ever seen a catfish any bigger, I don't

recollect it, 'cause he were somethin' to behold! I ain't lyin' when I say if he weren't thirty pound, he weren't nothin'!

Buster seen him and barked, 'cause he ain't never seen no fish *that* big. I think he were scared some. I looked old Spud Green in the eyes and says, "Howdy do, you old rascal?" And I almost expected him to say somethin' back, but he were tired as a fish could be, and he didn't say nothin'.

It took me and Buster three days to eat that fish, and he were real good with cornbread and taters.

Sometimes I wish I didn't catch him, 'cause I kind've miss him outdoin' me like he done. But, then, he were only a fish.

I think Mista Spud Green might've been bored that day I caught him. Maybe he were ready to make a choice. He just made the wrong one. I reckon there's the lesson.

Author's journal entry for September 3, 1966

I cut my finger real bad yesterday, so I poured some oil-o-sol in it and pulled it together with a band aid. But, today, I saw a red streak coming up my finger, so I went to find Fodder. He was sitting under his favorite tree by the river. I don't think he was feeling good because he didn't have his fishing pole, and he didn't tease me any when he saw me coming. He said the leaves on the trees were turning, and we might have a snowy winter. He didn't look good to me, but when I showed him my finger, he told me to come to the house, and when we got there, I saw a new grave in the yard. He said Buster had died, and he buried him there. Buster was a good dog, and I was sad. Fodder made a nice grave with river stones around it. He put some salve on my finger and said not to wrap it up. Then we sat on the porch, and he told me about when his wife, Bell, died. It made him real sad to say that, but he said you got to love people with everything in you while you have them. I wrote Fodder a little poem on some bark I pulled off a birch tree, and he liked it a lot. He said he'd always keep it. I got chilly when the wind started blowing, so when I got up I said, "You better get some wood on your pile for a snowy winter," because he always had a big wood pile beside the house, and there wasn't much there. He patted my shoulder and said, "You is a good young man." I don't think he's ever said my name. He calls me "boy" or "son" or "wild boy," because he doesn't know where I come from. But he said I'm like his own grandchild, and that makes me happy because I love Fodder like he's my own kin. He's a good man and takes time with a boy. I learn a lot of good things from my old friend.

Beneath the River Birches

I ain't never knowed what it were Bell seen in me. She were the pertiest thing I ever laid my eyes on, and she were educated, too! She knowed a lot of words and could tell you a story so it'd sound like she were readin' it from a book. And she were always readin' the Good Book around the house. That's how I know some of the things I know. But I give that woman a fit sometimes, 'cause she'd be a-readin' somethin' out loud, and I'd git to actin' like I were noddin' off, and, about then, I'd hear her say, "Fodda, are you listenin' or are you dreamin?" And I'd open my eyes big and shake my head like she done messed up my sleepin'. But then I'd give her the gist of what she said, and she'd smile a little and say, "You are always foolin' with me, Fodda, an' it's a good thing the Lord knows it."

I'd just chuckle and tell her to git on with it. But I ain't pullin' your leg, now. I never figured out what it were about me what kept her with me for so long a time.

Bell and me had a good life together. I don't mean it were always easy, 'cause it weren't. But if you put the good times in one bucket and the bad times in another one, then it'd be a chore to lift the good bucket.

I don't know. We just made the best of what the Lord sent our way, and tried not to fret none about what were around the bend. 'cause you cain't do nothin' about that, no way.

Bell did love to go places. Once the children were up and gone and I sold the mill, we were more able to git around the country and see relatives and all. My folks were in Tennessee and the Carolinas, and Bell had people in Georgia and Alabama. Whenever we'd go down South to visit, Bell would always like to see a show, 'cause she loved the music of the day. I were more fond of the spirituals. There were some musicians we seen that were real good. They were all black, 'cause you couldn't git in to see no white ones. We seen Bessie Smith, and she could make a bad song sound good. Ma Rainey even sung us a anniversary song one time when we were down in Georgia. We seen a lot of them, and some were blind. They called what they were doin' the blues, but it sure did make folks happy. I seen Sonny Boy Williamson once, and I were glad I did, 'cause he played the harmonica like nothin' I'd ever heard before.

All that were a long time ago, and for the last few years before Bell passed on, we stayed close to home in Virginia. It's always been real peaceful down here on the river.

Bell liked to go walkin' with me, and it weren't nothin' for that woman to come down here and sit with me while I were fishin' along the river bank. She'd read a book or write some of her poetry. But if I caught a fish, she'd make over it like it were somethin' real special. She were always sayin' a little somethin' what would make you feel good about yourself. Folks need to hear that from the ones who know them and love them.

It were real natural to hear Bell readin' or recitin' poetry with the sound of the river and the birds and the wind rustlin' the leaves of the birch trees. Old Buster would lay against her foot and be content as a bee in a honey jar.

One warm day in May of 1960, Bell come to me on the front porch and says, "Fodda, I want to take a walk with you down by the river."

Well, I looked at that woman and knowed she were sure wantin' to go. But she were right frail by then, and I were worried about her. She took my hand and said, "Fodda, it's all right."

It were a fine afternoon, and we seen the fish a-snappin' at the flies in the slow water. The new leaves on the maple trees and the river birches were about perty as I ever seen them, with the sun comin' through, all golden like it were.

Me and Bell moved along real slow, 'cause she were weak as a child, and I were worried. So I just held her close to me 'til we come to a big old maple tree on the bank what were at the bend in the river. It were a place I liked to sit sometimes and watch the river go by.

"Let's sit here," Bell said.

So I helped her to git comfortable against the tree before I sat down.

Then she leaned over to me 'til I were cradlin' her in my arms. I knowed it were her time, 'cause we both knowed it were comin'. She were so weak, and been sick in the heart for a long time.

I didn't know what to do, seein' her there a-lookin' at me the way she were. So I touched her face, and I says, "Bell, you the best woman I ever knowed, and I been blessed by the Almighty to have you."

She smiled then and whispered to me, "I love you, Fodda Milo," just as sweet as the day we were married.

Then I felt the life go out of her, and she laid there in my arms like she were sleepin'. So I says to her, "You just sleep, Bell. Old Fodder's here with you." But I were sad in my heart, and I were thinkin' why it were the birds kept a-singin' and the river kept a-flowin' by. It were like nothin' knowed I'd lost my Bell, 'cept me and Buster, 'cause he lifted his head, and I wondered if he'd seen her spirit go.

Well, we just sat there for a long time, me and Bell and Buster, 'cause I didn't want to git up. But then, I did. You got to keep on. Just like the birds a-singin' and the river a-flowin', and the wind. Bell told me that, and she were right.

Author's journal entry for October 14, 1966

Fodder Milo died last week. He was 94 years old. I had gone to visit him, but his children and some other people were at his house, and the one named Shad told me his daddy had died in his sleep. They knew about me and said Fodder wrote them letters and told them about the wild boy that was his friend. I ran all the way over to the old orchard on Sunday to his funeral. They buried him next to his wife and baby girl and sung some songs he liked. Shad said they put that little poem I wrote in his coat pocket, because he liked it a lot. I went to sit under Fodder's favorite tree by the river, but I didn't stay long, because it made me sad to think he is gone. I don't think I'll ever know another friend like Fodder Milo. I'm going to miss him forever.

Hills and Valleys

I seen a lot, 'cause I'm 94 year old. But I knowed folks who lived long lives and didn't see nothin'. You got to see what's around you all the time. And when the chance comes to step aboard somethin' new, you best take it. Sometimes it's right, and sometimes it ain't, but you're goin' to find out somethin' about yourself, and that's for sure!

I don't wish for much, now, 'cause the Lord's been good to me. But if I could have somethin' back, it'd be Bell and the children when they were

young 'uns. I miss them, laughin' and talkin' loud. I miss rhymin' with Anna on my knee. I miss my Bell, 'cause she sure were a fine woman.

A lifetime is full of hills and valleys, son. It's what you do between them hills and valleys that makes you the man you're goin' to be. Be ready for what the Lord'll send your way. Face all things with courage and dignity. Don't ever do or say nothin' to harm nobody, 'cause, in the end, you got yourself to live with.

I done been high and low, and I always done my best livin' between the hills and the valleys. Always.

The End

*Fodder Milo was one of the most admirable men I
have known. He was, to me, an American hero.
The stories you have read are my tribute to him.*

FEW

March 4, 2000

Titles by Francis Eugene Wood

The Wooden Bell (A Christmas Story)
The Legend of Chadega and the Weeping Tree
Wind Dancer's Flute
The Crystal Rose
The Angel Carver
The Fodder Milo Stories
The Nipkins (Trilogy)
Snowflake (A Christmas Story)
The SnowPeople (Trilogy)
Autumn's Reunion
The Teardrop Fiddle
Two Tales and a Pipe Dream

The books are available through the
author's website at tipofthemoon.com
or call (434) 392-5274.

Write to:
Tip-of-the-Moon Publishing Company
175 Crescent Road
Farmville, VA 23901

Francis Eugene Wood writes his stories from his home near Sheppards, Virginia, in Buckingham County. The award-winning author is known for his rich descriptions of rural Virginia life and his unique ability to blend fact and fiction in a way that mirrors the world around him. His books are released through Tip-of-the-Moon Publishing Company, a company he owns and operates with his wife, Chris.